PUFFIN BOOKS

Mudlark

As I sit here, waiting, I can smell the
fresh, black mud of Portsmouth Harbour.
I can feel it round my knees, cold
in summer, warm in winter.
Clinging and pulling me down, as if
it wanted me to be part of it.
As if it wanted to absorb me.
I loved it.

John Sedden is the pseudonym of a librarian who has worked in public, environmental, college and university libraries. Before becoming a librarian and writer, John was a civil servant, a gardener, a factory labourer, a cardboard box maker, a househusband and a teacher. He lives on the south coast with his wife, Irene, and daughter, Karen.

Books by John Sedden

MUDLARK

Mudlark

John Sedden

To Ken
with very best wishes
to an ex-mudlark!

John Sedden

PUFFIN

PUFFIN BOOKS

Published by the Penguin Group
Penguin Books Ltd, 80 Strand, London WC2R 0RL, England
Penguin Group (USA) Inc., 375 Hudson Street, New York, New York 10014, USA
Penguin Group (Canada), 10 Alcorn Avenue, Toronto, Ontario, Canada M4V 3B2
(a division of Pearson Penguin Canada Inc.)
Penguin Ireland, 25 St Stephen's Green, Dublin 2, Ireland (a division of Penguin Books Ltd)
Penguin Group (Australia), 250 Camberwell Road,
Camberwell, Victoria 3124, Australia (a division of Pearson Australia Group Pty Ltd)
Penguin Books India Pvt Ltd, 11 Community Centre,
Panchsheel Park, New Delhi – 110 017, India
Penguin Group (NZ), cnr Airborne and Rosedale Roads, Albany,
Auckland 1310, New Zealand (a division of Pearson New Zealand Ltd)
Penguin Books (South Africa) (Pty) Ltd, 24 Sturdee Avenue,
Rosebank 2196, South Africa

Penguin Books Ltd, Registered Offices: 80 Strand, London WC2R 0RL, England

www.penguin.com

First published 2005
1

Set in 11.5/15 pt Monotype Bembo
Typeset by Rowland Phototypesetting Ltd, Bury St Edmunds, Suffolk
Made and printed in England by Clays Ltd, St Ives plc

British Library Cataloguing in Publication Data
A CIP catalogue record for this book is available from the British Library

ISBN 0–141–31868–6

For Irene

Chapter One

Do you ever wonder how you ended up where you are? If you're anything like me, you only do it when things go wrong. When you're in a bit of a hole. Well, I'm doing it right now. Wondering how I ended up where I am. Because, as holes go, the one I'm in couldn't be bigger.

I have to write it down, to explain how it ended like this.

Not for anyone else, but for me. I guess I want to explain it to myself.

But I hope someone else reads it as well, because it could be the only thing left.

I don't know if I've got time to write it all down.

It's nearly time.

As I sit here, waiting, I can smell the fresh, black mud of Portsmouth Harbour. I can feel it round my knees, cold in summer, warm in winter. Clinging and pulling me down, as if it wanted me to be part of it. As if it wanted to absorb me.

I loved it.

Loved its feel as I waded through it. Slimy and gritty at the same time. Smooth and scratchy. It didn't want to let go of you when you came home. It stuck to you like a second layer of thick skin, and by the time you reached Jubilee Terrace it had dried into a grey crust. As you walked home you become aware of its weight. Gradually it crazed and broke round your knees and ankles and elbows and wrists.

If Mum had company, I'd sit on the kerb and pick at my legs and try and get bigger and bigger scabs off. But it would always crumble to nothing between my fingers at the last minute, just when I thought I'd done it. Always. Like it was some law of nature.

Mum wasn't so keen on the black mud of Portsmouth Harbour. I'd creep round the alley and come in the back way. But she'd always catch me, point the finger and say, 'You been mudlarkin' again, don't deny it.'

There I was, black up to my waist as if I'd been dipped in treacle.

She'd look stern, but she knew I knew that she wasn't really angry. It was our, like, joke.

'Yeah, Mum. How can you tell?'

'An educated guess, ya cheeky beggar. You've brought 'alf the bleedin' 'arbour mud back wiv ya. And made a million winkles 'omeless!'

It was always winkles or cockles or whelks. They took it in turns whenever Mum told me off. I imagined them in the harbour looking round for their home, looking for their mud.

'It was here a minute ago,' one would say.

'Yeah, that was before Jimmy arrived,' another would reply bitterly, shaking his head, or whatever shellfish shake when they're bitter.

Mum smiled as she helped peel off my shirt and trousers, starched stiff with dried mud. She pulled the tin bath off the backyard wall and dropped it on to the cobbles. It clattered as it spun and settled, announcing to all our neighbours in Jubilee Terrace what I'd been up to. Nobody used their baths on a weekday unless they had to.

Mum'd go and fetch the scrubbing brush and carbolic soap. Those brushes were murder when they were new. Mum got them for free from a friend who was high-up at Palmer's brush factory. Once they'd been broken in and the bristles had softened they weren't so bad. She'd hand me the brush and start the relay of steaming jugs of hot water from the kitchen range. I'd sit there, in the tub in my underpants, pleased that our backyard had such high walls. I'd unclench my fist and drop the mud-encrusted coins one by one into the tub and start rubbing them between my fingers. I'd guess which royal head would appear – Vic, Ted or George – but I'd always, always, always get it wrong. Funny really. One-in-three chance. Another of those laws of nature, I suppose.

★

4

Mum'd ask, 'How much d'ya make?'

It varied. Sometimes as little as thruppence.* Sometimes as much as two bob or even half a crown.

Whatever it was, it didn't matter, she'd say, 'Good lad. You're a good lad, Jimmy.'

She'd pour the hot water down my back. I can feel it now. Washing away my sins.

Mum would say, 'All you need is a few jugfuls to wash away yours, Jimmy lad. I'm beyond 'elp, me. It'd take all the water in the 'arbour to wash mine away!'

And she'd laugh.

She didn't really mind me mudlarking. She pretended to, but we needed the money and she knew I loved it. It was my contribution and it meant she wouldn't have to work so hard.

Mum worked as a casual barmaid, doing a few hours here and there, whenever a pub in the area was short-staffed or extra busy. Working that way, Mum made a lot of friends, but I didn't like her doing it. It meant she drank more. And most of the money she earned went back on the gin.

I knew she didn't like doing what she did either.

But we never talked about it.

Mum's work was one of those things you just didn't talk about.

* There is a guide to old money on page 247.

The other thing we never talked about was my dad.
My dad who I'd never met.

I'd finish washing the ha'pennies and pennies and put
them in neat piles on the wet cobbles beside the tub. Then
I'd ask Mum to scrub my back where I couldn't reach.

I can smell the carbolic in the steam and feel the bristles
taking off the mud and scratching me in that place in
the middle of your back that you can't reach. Sometimes
it felt so good and other times I'd scream blue murder.
Mum would laugh and that would set me off screaming
and laughing at the same time. It was like a reward and a
punishment for what I'd brought home. The reward for
the coins and the punishment for the mud.

We were the mudlarks. That's what we did for a
living. Some people called us dirty beggars. Told us to
stop scrounging. Told us to go and get a job.

Now I can't deny we were dirty, but we weren't
beggars. And there was no need to go and get a job,
because we had one. Mudlarking.

By 'we' I mean me and my mates. Reg lived opposite
in Jubilee Terrace. He was my best mate. He had a stutter
which came and went. When it came, it took him twice
as long to say what he had to say. And when it went,
he talked twice as much sense and was twice as funny as
anyone else. Other kids took the p-p-piss, but he could
look after himself. His mum used to work the same as my
mum until she chucked it in after getting beaten up. She

went and got a job in Voller's corset factory off Queen's Street. Me and Reg had a lot in common. We were both mad keen on Pompey (that's Portsmouth FC). Neither of us knew who our dads were. And we were both mudlarks.

I'd been thinking a lot about my dad that summer. Sometimes I'd see a man who might look a bit like me and wonder if he was my dad. It's stupid, really. I mean, what are the chances? I asked Reg whether he ever thought about stuff like that.

'Naah, Jimmy. Waste of f-f-flippin' time,' he shrugged. 'My d-d-dad was one of me mum's customers when she was working round the pubs, so n-n-nobody knows who he is.'

Reg had a lot of common sense. In fact, looking back at what happened, I think he must have got my share when it was being doled out.

'But don't you ever wonder what he was like?'

Reg shook his head and looked at me suspiciously. I had to explain.

'I mean, sometimes, do you ever wonder who you are, cos of not knowin' where you come from? Do you know what I mean, Reg?'

Reg looked at me blankly.

'Nope, c-c-can't say I do. But if you ever f-f-forget who you are, just ask. I'll p-p-put ya right, Jimmy!'

We laughed, but I had a feeling that Reg knew what I meant. It's funny. You don't think about things like that when you're a little kid. You've got your mum and that's enough. But when you're fourteen you start wondering.

At the beginning of August, when the Huns invaded poor old Belgium, we'd declared war. By we, I mean Great Britain. Not me and Reg.

'Where the f-f-flippin' heck is Belgium?' asked Reg when we heard Jop shout the news from his pitch on the railway pier. He was surrounded by customers, expertly delivering folded newspapers with one hand and collecting pennies with the other.

He'd put his Crimean War medals on special and polished up his Sunday-best wooden leg, even though it was a Tuesday.

I pushed through the crowd and waved a penny, but he brushed it aside. 'Have this one on me, Jimmy son. I'm havin' a good day. It's great news, ain't it! I've sold over three hundred papers so far today!'

I smiled and took the paper, and Reg and I wandered down to the foreshore, reading aloud as we went. 'Following the assassination of the Austrian archduke . . . blah, blah, blah . . . Germany invades Belgium . . . blah, blah, blah . . . Britain's ultimatum to withdraw is ignored . . . blah, blah, blah . . . the Empire is at war.'

Reg and I stood in the mud and looked up at the pier hopefully, but nobody was going to toss us coins today. They were all going to Jop.

'What I want to know is, where the f-f-flippin' heck is Belgium?' repeated Reg, unable to understand what the fuss was about and aggrieved at his loss of earnings.

'Dunno,' I shrugged. 'Abroad.'

'Thanks, Jimmy. Thanks very much. Very f-f-flippin' informative. I'll add that to my s-s-store of geography knowledge.' He held his head and closed his eyes as if straining to absorb my pathetic fact.

Sometimes Reg's sarcasm made me angry, and this was one of those times. I grabbed a handful of mud, cupped it into a ball and slung it. I knew it was a good one, the second it left my hand. Straight, square on Reg's forehead, with force enough to knock him back, flat, into the mud. It was one of those perfect shots that you have to apologize for because it was just so damn perfect.

'Sorry, Reg.' I tried to not laugh. ' I didn't mean . . .'

'You b-b-bustard! This is war!'

Reg was thrashing about on his back like an upturned crab, sinking deeper in the mud.

'You f-f-f . . .!' He gave up thrashing and started laughing. Reg was a good sport.

I waded over to pull him up, smiling, offering my hand. Reg was completely covered in pitch-black mud. If it wasn't for his eyes and mouth you wouldn't know he was there.

The yank on my arm should have been expected, but it wasn't and I joined him in the mud.

So you can see why we were best mates. Not so much blood-brothers as mud-brothers. Our friendship sworn and sealed in the mud of Portsmouth Harbour.

How did the war begin? Jop tried to explain once but didn't get very far. Apparently this kid shot Archduke

Ferdinand of Austria (Reg and I mouthed the word 'Who?' to each other) and this led to Germany invading Belgium. Yeah, I know, we didn't get it either. Anyway, because of that daft kid, Pompey didn't have much of a side cos all the best players had gone off to fight. Me and Reg reckoned we ought to offer our services, but we knew they'd say no and laugh at us because of our age. By 'offer our services', I meant play soccer for our team, Pompey, not fight the bloody Germans. Me and Reg weren't that stupid.

Some of our mates' dads had joined the army. Posters appeared one day on postboxes, shop windows and bill-boards with a picture of Lord Kitchener pointing a huge, chubby finger. 'Your country needs YOU,' it said.

Me and Reg first saw it pasted up over the South Gate of Fratton Park as we queued up at the turnstile. We stared up at it and Lord Kitchener stared back, accusingly.

'I wonder if old K-K-Kitchener picks 'is nose with that finger.'

'Course he does. Everyone picks their nose.'

'What, even the K-K-King?'

'Especially the King. What else has he got to do except pose for postage stamps?'

Reg nodded and gazed back.

'With a f-f-finger that size K-K-Kitchener must have nostrils as wide as a G-G-Gunwharf cannon.'

'Must be lethal when he sneezes.'

★

We paid our thruppence at the turnstile and stood on the terrace to watch another sound thrashing. West Ham outclassed us totally, and the crowd was pathetic. A few hundred old men and kids. What sort of support is that? Where were the four thousand other regulars? It was the war, of course. If they hadn't joined up, they were working sixteen hours a day in the Dockyard. Some of our mates never saw their dads any more because they left home before dawn and didn't came back until after dark.

It might sound nasty, but Reg and I were sort of pleased that Belgium had been invaded because it meant we were all the same now. None of us had dads. We were all equal.

It was a shame about poor old Pompey, though. And Belgium. Wherever it is.

'P-P-P-Pompey needs US,' said Reg in a toffee voice, pointing at me and trying to look stern like Kitchener. He'd smeared some mud under his nose to look like he had Kitchener's thick moustache. You had to use your imagination, but it sort of worked.

'Yeah, Reg. One day they'll come knockin' at my door, pleadin'.'

I ought to explain, I was a better player than Reg.

Kitchener's finger pointed up to the sky.

'W-w-what's that?'

I followed the finger and looked up at an empty sky.

'What? Where?'

Kitchener's eyes narrowed.

'In the distance. Is it a Z-Z-Zeppelin?'

'Where?' I blinked to refocus.

'Or is it a . . . yes, I think it's a . . . p-p-pig.'

I punched Lord Kitchener and gave him the mother of dead arms.

One good thing, the war meant a bit more money, at least when the reservists and volunteers started arriving in Portsmouth to be trained and shipped off to the war. Mum got more work in the pubs to cope with the demand, and us mudlarks didn't do badly either.

Let me explain. Every day we went down to the fresh mud in the harbour between the Hard and the railway pier where the steam engines brought the sailors and soldiers from London. They were all keen because they'd just volunteered.

If you stood under the pier when a train arrived, you could tell if it was packed or not. The more men in the carriages, the deeper the rumble. Lately there had been lots of deep rumbles. Then they'd clatter off back to London or wherever, to pick up more.

The men were proud and excited and smart in their new uniforms. Rich pickings. Most of the sailors (bluejackets), marines (joeys) and soldiers (Tommies) had heard of us. We were famous. One of the sights of Portsmouth. The eighth wonder of the bleedin' world.

I guess we were entertainers, really. Before the war we entertained the excursionists, the holidaymakers who always had pocketfuls of loose change for souvenirs and tacky pleasures. For one coin the thrower enjoyed the spectacle of yours truly racing and fighting his mates in the mud to retrieve the coin. And we all put on a show, diving and clowning and messing around like Charlie Chaplin did every week at the Coliseum Picture House. Before the war it seemed to be prim old ladies who enjoyed us the most. Reg reckoned it was because they'd spent their lives being so stuck-up, stuffy and starched that they secretly wanted to strip off, undo their corsets and roll around in the mud starkers.

The foreshore – the mud between high and low tide – was our stage. After it had been washed by the tide, the mud was smooth and its shiny surface unbroken. We'd race in, making footprints then heavy gouges as we waded in deeper and deeper, pocking and scarring the surface. It was like we were the dirt and the mud was clean.

Then one of us would cup his hands round his mouth and shout up. Since the war it had been, 'Throw us a shillin', sir!' if it was an officer. Or, 'Chuck us a tanner, mister!' if it was bluejacket, joey or Tommy. Or, 'Spare us a penny, matey!' if it was a Dockyard worker.

Sometimes, if it was an officer with a really posh lady, we'd pitch for half a crown, but it was rare to get anything silver, especially that big. You got more if the soldier or sailor was courting a lady, because he'd want to impress. That's how we made the real money. I guess it could look a bit like begging, except it wasn't really because we earned it. And, of course, there was the occasional perk.

You see, you never knew what the tide would bring in. Sometimes treasure, like the time Archie found a real gold wedding ring. It had more carrots than the Beresford allotments! He took it up Berlusconi's, the pawnbroker in Queen's Street, and got two crisp ten-bob notes for it.

And you could get a week's worth of firewood when the Dockyard carpenters ditched their off-cuts in the harbour. And sometimes, if the navy had been testing their mines and torpedoes up harbour, you'd get dozens of fish washed up, which took care of your suppers for a week. You had to be careful, though, and check inside the gills to see how long they'd been dead.

But sometimes there was horrible stuff. Like turds from the sewage pipes and ships' sluices. Or stiff, dead rats two foot long. Or putrid guts from the navy's slaughterhouse over Gosport. Nasty stuff.

No, you never knew what the tide would deliver.

One day – it was Wednesday the twenty-third of September – that day, Reg found a human skull.

Chapter Two

That was what started it all. That skull.

I spotted a bluejacket with a kitbag on his back, swaggering along the railway pier.

I cupped my hands and shouted up, 'Chuck us a tanner, Jack!'

'You'll be lucky, yer little beggar!' he laughed, pulling his hand out of his pocket. He studied what he held, selected a coin and skimmed it out into the distance, far out into the deep harbour mud, scattering some seagulls that were paddling and feeding on the water's edge.

Reg never did any shouting up, because of his stutter, but he had a keen, cormorant's eye. This gave him the edge when it came to long-distance throws. He could estimate the distance and direction with pin-point accuracy.

The race was on.

Against my mates.

Against time.

Get it before anyone else.

Get it before it sank.

The further out you got, the deeper the mud, and the harder it became. Like running uphill with a grapnel anchor chained to each ankle. That really gets the crowd laughing.

That day there were only four of us. Apart from Reg and me, there was Archie and his kid sis, Lillie, who he looked after. Even though she was only little, Lillie was like a Dreadnought's anchor so far as Archie was concerned, though he never showed it. One thing he could do was mudlarking, because Lillie loved the mud too. Archie always sat her next to one of the thick oak struts that supported the railway pier and showed her how to finger-draw in the shallow mud, and put together huge mud pies for her rag-doll.

Lillie was a clever kid. She'd named her rag-doll Lillie, and never let it out of her sight. This was useful because, whenever she was getting told off, Lillie would always blame it on rag-doll-Lillie. You can only get away with stuff like that when you're little.

Though he was soft with his kid sis, when it came to mudlarking Archie was as tough as a joey's old boots. Pushing or elbows was OK, but punching was foul play. These were the rules. If the coin landed flat, the crater stayed for a few seconds before filling itself in. Those few seconds gave you a chance. If it slipped into the mud sideways, you were likely scuppered. You had to guess where it had entered and the angle of entry and plunge your hand in, deeper and deeper, groping for that hard, round, smooth coin before it was lost forever.

Archie and I knew that Reg had this one in the bag. We followed him far out into the Harbour, but he was too fast and sure of where it fell. He plunged his arm in, pulled it out and studied it suspiciously.

'A f-f-f-farthin'! The miserable g-g-g-git!'

We laughed and Reg joined in.

It was then that he noticed the human skull.

It was lying on the edge of the water, gleaming white against the black mud. Reg gave a shout and beckoned to us with his black arm. We waded out further, gathering around, gradually realizing what it was, not daring to get too close. Reg picked up a bit of driftwood, leant forward and poked it.

Suddenly there was a scratching, scurrying sound.

The skull started moving.

Jesus.

You could have heard us scream on the other side of the harbour. I'll bet we were louder than the Dockyard whistle. We freeze. The skull starts moving, and we're up to our knees in mud, unable to get away, to create some distance. Then Archie laughs nervously. I turn my head and see dozens of green-and-orange crabs spilling out through the eye sockets. Their little legs gently tap against the bone, and the skull amplifies the sound of their frantic escape.

That noise is everything I can hear, and I imagine them rattling around in my own skull, gripping and twisting with their pincers, feasting on my brain and eyes.

I hear myself breathe out and say at the same time, 'Bloody 'ell!'

Reg pokes my shoulder with his stick and makes me jump out of my skin.

'You thought it was still alive, ya j-j-j-jessie!'

'So did you, ya bustard.'

I don't like being touched by the stick after it had touched the skull. But I don't say anything.

We stare silently at the shiny-wet, grinning skull. The crabs disappear into a clump of slimy, flowing bladder-wrack that lay strewn beside it like an old wig.

I don't know how long we stood there. It was one of those moments when you don't feel real, when you seem to be aware of everything and nothing. The gentle, lapping rhythm of the sea changed. The tide was starting to turn.

We looked at each other. Nobody knew what to say. It was strange. It was like we were embarrassed. Like we had seen something we shouldn't. Something wrong or bad had happened, and we had found the evidence.

We trudged back to Lillie, who was happily ignorant of our find.

It was Reg who spoke what was on our minds.

'Sh-sh-sh-shouldn't we tell someone?'

Two thoughts occurred. Firstly, we didn't want to be cuffed round the ear'ole by the coppers for begging.

Because that's what they called mudlarking. They didn't think we were the eighth wonder. They thought we were scum.

Second, we didn't want to get locked up and hung for murder either. If there was one thing you learnt early in Portsea, it was never trust the police. Ever. Given half a chance, they'd stitch you up tighter than a kipper's corset and throw away the needle.

'Yeah, Reg,' I said reluctantly, ' I suppose we're gonna have to tell someone.'

Archie picked up Lillie and her rag-doll.

'Lillie loves mud poise,' said Lillie, clutching rag-doll-Lillie.

'So she does,' said Archie, looking at a dense black mud ball underneath which, somewhere, was rag-doll-Lillie's head.

'And I loves Lillie,' said Lillie, kissing the dense black mud ball. She looked expectantly at Archie, with mud on her face.

'And I loves Lillie,' mumbled Archie, kissing his sister on her forehead.

Reg and I exchanged a grimace.

We climbed up over the glistening bladderwrack, popping them under our bare feet, up on to the cobbled Hard.

The road outside the Dockyard Gates was bustling with bluejackets heading for their ships. Hundreds of dockies on shiftwork were coming in fresh or going home weary.

The war had brought the streets of Portsea to life, and at the heart of it was the Dockyard, busily building warships to teach the Hun a lesson. That lesson was that our warships are bigger and better. And that we rule the waves.

Archie shouted 'Tarra!' and disappeared with Lillie into the crowd. Me and Reg were going to be the good citizens.

I spotted a copper chatting up a lady outside the Keppel's Head and pointed him out to Reg.

Reg nodded thoughtfully and stopped a little boy who was skipping by. He whispered in his ear and slipped the sailor's farthing into his tiny palm. The boy polished the coin up on his ragged shirt, inspected it, smiled and skipped over to the pub. We watched as he tugged on the copper's sleeve. The copper brushed him away, but the boy persisted and eventually the copper stooped down to hear what he had to say. The boy pointed and the copper looked out into the harbour mud, disappointed that he was going to have to do something about this.

Reg and I sat on an upturned rowing boat and watched as he marched down the cobbled Hard. He gingerly untied his boots, slipped off his socks and climbed down the slimy bladderwrack into the mud, cursing at every step.

When he was safely down in the mud, Reg and I looked at the boots and then at each other. The same thing crossed our minds. It was our telepathy.

'Naah,' we said, shaking our heads.

We fell silent for a few minutes as the policeman made

his way towards the skull, but our gazes kept returning to those boots.

'We could have them away, no sweat.'

Reg nodded.

'Yeah, b–b–but it wouldn't be r–r–right, would it?'

'No, but it's fine leather, nicely broken in,' I observed. 'Call me fussy, but I don't fancy the socks.'

'No,' agreed Reg. 'It's b–b–been very hot this morning.'

We watched as the copper reached the skull and stooped over it, studying it closely. He drew his truncheon from his trousers and poked it, just as Reg had done. Suddenly he shouted, jumped back, lost his balance and fell into the mud. His helmet rolled off and settled next to the skull. All Reg and I could hear was swearing and the desperate sounds of suction as he tried to pull himself out. Reg and I laughed and laughed until we could taste salt from the tears.

'A copper mudlarkin'! That's w–w–worth a tanner of anyone's m–m–money!'

I put on my best straight face.

'You can laugh, Reg, but we've got some serious competition here. They could put us out of business!'

That creased Reg up and when I see Reg crease up, I crease up worse.

The policeman struggled back on to the Hard, still swearing, his uniform caked in mud. He pulled his whistle out of his breast pocket and put it to his lips. Five short blasts called for help.

We knew the coppers' whistle code. We'd grown up with it. They had different patterns for different crimes. But five short blasts was a new one on me and Reg.

If us mudlarks were the eighth wonder of the world, the ninth has to be the sight of Portsea's coppers running down from their station in Queen's Street whenever there was a drunken brawl in the pubs on the Hard. This happens at least once a day, usually when a Tommy has insulted a bluejacket or a bluejacket has insulted a Tommy. It didn't matter who started it, the result was the same. Two long blasts on a whistle, reinforcements, truncheons, broken bones. It was almost better sport than watching Pompey.

Those coppers aren't built for speed. Especially since all the younger ones had joined up and been replaced by old men who were too clapped out to fight in the war.

That's one thing that always creases me and Reg up. I think it's got something to do with the red, gasping faces underneath those smart, tall, blue helmets with the carefully polished silver badge in the middle.

An elderly constable puffed past us, barely faster than walking pace, one hand keeping his helmet on, the other clutching his heavy truncheon. I waited until he was out of earshot.

'If he doesn't hurry up, the tide will have come and gone and ferried the skull off to the Isle of Wight.'

Reg laughed. 'If he was an 'orse, he'd be put out of his m-m-m-misery down the knacker's yard!'

I smiled.

'Perhaps that's what happens to old coppers. They don't retire. They get poleaxed and end up in old Grubb's sausages.'

'I love old Grubb's s-s-s-sausages,' Reg laughed, and he punched me in the arm. 'That's for s-s-s-spoilin' every one I eat from now on.'

You'll have gathered that we didn't much like coppers. We usually took the piss out of them between ourselves, but that's as far as it went. What made it different that day was the skull. This was serious. We'd never seen a human skull before. Not for real. To be honest, it shook us up a bit, though we tried to hide it.

'It's like s-s-s-someone who's really, really, very, very bald,' said Reg. We stared out at the shiny-wet white dome that stood out from the mud. 'I reckons it was likely a German s-s-s-spy, sent to collect information on the Dockyard and the f-f-f-fortifications round the 'arbour.'

'Yeah, he could have drowned while trying to swim to the shore from a U-boat . . .'

'Or been s-s-s-sliced up by a sh-sh-sh-ship's propellors,' added Reg with relish.

More coppers arrived and gathered around the skull, staring and pointing. There were now seven pairs of black leather boots standing on the Hard, just waiting to go for a walk. There was bound to be two pairs that fitted me and Reg. I nodded towards them with my 'we'd be silly not to' look, but Reg looked disgusted.

'You're t-t-terrible, you. You'd take advantage of this s-s-situation to get yerself a pair of b-b-boots?'

Sometimes Reg turned into his mother, and this was one of those times. But when he looked down at his bare feet, I could tell he was tempted. Who wouldn't be? The thing was, Reg and I didn't have any boots or shoes. We always went barefoot. Only kids with dads had boots, and there weren't many of them in Portsea. In Southsea, the posh bit of Portsmouth, every kid had boots. Reg once said that even babies in prams wore them, but that sounded too mad to be true.

We all told ourselves that going barefoot is what nature intended, at least that's what our mums told us. And that's a fair point. I mean, I don't know of any animals that wear boots. I suppose there're the tradesmen's carthorses with their horseshoes nailed to their feet by the smithy, but you couldn't say that was natural.

'You're right,' I said, nodding and looking back in the direction of the skull. Reg breathed a sigh of relief. 'Thank g-g-goodness for that. You know I d-d-don't like pinchin' stuff.'

'No, Reg. I meant you're right. You can't get much balder than that skull.'

We watched in silence as the policemen strutted about as best they could in the mud, looking at the skull from different angles and offering each other their opinions. Suddenly, a motor car turned in from the road, making me and Reg jump, as it clattered down the cobbled Hard. It braked at the end and a man in a dark suit climbed out. He was holding a black leather bag. Good quality. Very expensive. It reminded me of a doctor's bag, except it was a bit bigger and more posh. The suit took off his shoes, awkwardly rolled up his trouser legs and clambered down to join the coppers. He tried to look important and dignified, but it just isn't possible when you're knee-deep in our mud.

'Is he a d-d-doctor? 'S bit late for a d-d-doctor.'

'Naah, I reckon he's one of them paf-olly-jists. He gets a bundle of money for declarin' that people is dead.'

'Well I c-c-could do that,' said Reg, staring at the skull. 'I c-c-could do that easily. I could do that from 'ere.'

Seven pairs of boots, and now a pair of expensive, hand-made shoes. All waiting to be taken for a walk. Chances like this didn't come along very often. There had to be something there that fitted Reg and me. And Archie. And probably some of the other lads.

Reg shifted his gaze back to his feet.

I worked on him a bit more. 'Look at it this way, Reg. We won't be doin' any mudlarkin' today. Them boots there are like an offer of compensation for the money we ain't earnin'. Them coppers have occupied our mud. We're entitled.'

Reg shook his head.

'Oh, come on, Reg! You know you want to! One of

them pairs has got your name on. Remember last winter when we got stuck to the ice on the Hard cos we stood still for too long?'

Reg nodded. I could tell from his face that he remembered only too well. It wasn't just the pain, it was the humiliation: the passers-by pointing and laughing as we struggled to free ourselves without losing the skin off the soles of our feet.

No. Going barefoot in winter was no joke. On really cold days your feet went blue, even if you wrapped them up in strips of old blanket. And then the pain came when they warmed up. Bad pain. Pain that made you wish you were dead.

Reg knew all this. But I'm telling you, so that you'll understand. I'm not making excuses for what happened. I'm just trying to tell you the way it was.

Reg groaned to himself. He didn't like dilemmas.

'Think about it, Reg. There'd be no more staring at the pavement, worrying about hot fag-ends or broken glass or dog crap. You could walk proud and look people in the eye with a pair of boots on. Just like a proper gent.'

A flicker of a smile crossed Reg's face. He was softening.

'You're a b-b-bad influence, Jimmy.'

Reg had turned into his mother again, but it didn't last long. He stopped thinking and smiled and nodded.

'Let's d-d-do it.'

Chapter Three

We slid down off the boat and sauntered down the Hard like we were having a nonchalant stroll, taking the sea air, like you do. The coppers were preoccupied helping the important suit, who was measuring the skull with a tape measure.

We reached the car and bent down as if we were taking a break from our nonchalant stroll to do up our boot laces. Nonchalantly. Like you do.

Not that we had any boots on. At least not yet. One by one we grabbed the trailing laces and clenched them in our fists. Stuffed into the boots were fourteen sweaty socks. They looked like they'd got holes in, but if they were for ventilation it wasn't working. The stench hit our nostrils. Reg's eyes started to water and I switched off my nose and breathed through my mouth.

'We'll lose them later,' I hissed.

'Pref'rably s-s-sooner,' said Reg. I could tell he was on the brink of changing his mind again.

'Ready?' I whispered.

'S-s-s'pose s-s-so. What about the paff-olly-git's s-s-shoes?'

'No, leave 'em. Pinching from coppers is one thing. Besides, we'd soon get picked up, walkin' round Portsea in them fancy things.'

I checked the escape route up the Hard to Queen's Street.

'Ready?'

Reg nodded.

'Go!'

We were up and away from the harbour like an inshore force nine. The boots swung on their laces like mad clappers. A deep voice far behind in the mud shouted, 'Oy!', another, 'Stop!' A whistle sounded, shrill and piercing. Two long blasts. Theft.

The whistle had given its verdict. Reg and I were thieves!

I felt that stuff in my blood; that stuff that pumps round and round and makes you fly like a thief. But no.

We weren't thieves.

Not unless we were caught.

And that stuff in our blood wasn't going to let that happen.

No chance.

The whistle would have alerted any coppers at the station and they'd be puffing their way down Queen's Street to grab us.

No chance. Not in a century of Sundays.

You see, Reg and I are quick. Damned quick. Our legs go like pistons. We don't look back. That's the golden rule. Never look back.

★

I was ahead of Reg, but I heard his feet slapping the ground behind me. Fog Corner and the Dockyard Gate flashed past. We reached Queen's Street and ran in the gutter, avoiding the shoppers and sailors on the narrow pavement. We dodged a tram. The driver shouted out of his window but the clatter of his tram drowned his words. We slipped into Rourke's Passage to avoid the reinforcements and Reg gasped directions, 'Left 'ere! . . . Right there! . . . Over the wall!' and so on, deeper and deeper into the dark network of Portsea alleys that Reg and I know like the back of our eyelids. A gang of kids parted to let us through, their eyes following the coppers' bouncing boots with envy. They would block the alley behind us, ready to deny all knowledge.

Brown rats scattered from rubbish heaps and dis-appeared in an instant. Dogs barked from behind locked gates. A ginger tom on top of a wall opened his eyes, then closed them again.

A lady was hanging out her washing on a line stretched zig-zag across the alley. It drooped too low to duck.

The line snapped on my chest. I won the race!

'Bleedin' 'ooligans!'

My prize was a pair of the lady's huge bloomers that clung to my front. I heard Reg laugh as I peeled them off, so I chucked them over my shoulder at him, but he ducked and blew me a kiss in triumph. Left again, then right, then we stopped round the back of Archie's place.

'I r-r-reckon we're s-s-safe now,' gasped Reg as he bent over, putting his hands on his knees to catch his breath. My heart was beating hard and fast.

'No sign of the plods! They're probably still trying to get out of the mud!'

Reg smiled. 'Well, they ain't called p-p-plods fer no reason.'

We looked at each other and then at the boots in our hands and we laughed.

'Let's go in and show Archie. He'll be made up.'

Archie's kitchen was thick with steam. He was standing over the stove, boiling an egg for Lillie's tea, and Lillie was on the kitchen floor, getting rag-doll–Lillie's tea.

'Hey, how's it goin'?' Archie asked, filling up the kettle to make a brew. 'Did you tell the coppers about the skull?'

'Sort of, Archie. And we found these.'

Reg and I held up the bunches of boots proudly, like they were prized fruit scrumped from Mr Mott's orchard.

'Bloody 'ell!' said Archie, with eyes as round as a surprised halibut.

'Bloody 'ell!' repeated Lillie.

'Take yer p-p-pick!' We laid them out on the kitchen table and sat down to examine them.

'Where'd they come from?'

'Someone just left 'em lying there on the Hard,' I explained.

Reg looked at me and smiled.

'Well, it's true,' I argued.

Reg explained the full story to Archie, who looked horrified but then laughed.

'You must be mad. They'll flippin' murder yer!'

'They'll 'ave to catch us first.'

Reg was peering into each boot one by one and dividing them up into pairs.

'Where's the s-s-socks? They've g-g-gone.'

Reg was right. There was no smell.

'They must have jigged out while we was running.'

The boots were now sorted into pairs.

Archie chose some and held one against his foot.

'They're a bit, like, big, aren't they?'

He was right. They were all big. In fact they were all enormous.

Reg bagged the pair that seemed smaller than the others, pulled them on and stood up. 'These are useless. It's like I'm s-s-standing in two f-f-flippin' buckets.' He looked at me accusingly. 'You and your b-b-bleedin' b-b-bright ideas!'

Reg sat down and held his head in his hands.

'Stuff 'em,' I suggested. 'Stuff 'em with scrunched-up newspaper.'

'Stuff 'em!' repeated Lillie as she dropped rag-doll-Lillie in a boot so that only her head was visible.

Archie fetched an old newspaper and Reg scrunched up some pages, padded out the boots and stood up again.

'Well?'

'Naah. Now it's like s-s-standin' in two buckets with s-s-scrunched-up newspapers.'

There was a long silence while Lillie bounced rag-doll-Lillie around the kitchen floor, using the bootlaces like puppet strings.

'I suppose we could flog 'em,' I suggested, trying

to save face. 'We'd get a few bob fer 'em down the pawnies.'

Mum sometimes sent me down to Berlusconi's before the war when she wasn't getting any work and there was no food or gin in the house. Mr Berlusconi's pawnshop was on the corner of Albert Street. His window was crammed with medals and jewellery, watches, corsets and clothing, and if you looked carefully you could see a pair of false teeth, two different-coloured glass eyes and lots of other weird things. This junk and treasure was protected from smash-and-grab merchants by a thick wire mesh that covered the window.

'And how did you come by these?'

Reg nudged me to answer. He knew I had a better imagination. Or that I was a better liar.

'They belonged to me brothers. They don't need 'em any more. They've grown out of 'em. So they asked me to sell 'em fer a good price.'

Mr Berlusconi looked into my eyes. I wouldn't believe me either, but I held his stare and passed the boots through the bars that protected Mr Berlusconi from his customers. He felt the quality of the leather and checked the stitching on the seams, shaking his head. He always shook his head at whatever he was looking at. It was his way of telling you that you weren't going to get much for it.

He then turned them towards the light from the window to examine the wear on the soles. He grunted and placed them back on the counter.

'Your brothers, what do they do for a living?'

'They work in the Dockyard,' I said, looking him straight in the eyes. What's it got to do with him, anyway? He looked me up and down and sighed, and I realized I was still covered in mud and probably looked a bit suspicious.

'These boots. They have the words "Police Property" stamped on the instep. This suggests to me that they are the property of the police.'

I sensed Reg leaving my side and shuffling backwards towards the door.

'I'll just go and talk to my brothers about it,' I said weakly. 'Goodbye.'

Reg already had the door open, and we were gone before you could say 'stolen property'.

We headed home, minus the boots and with nothing else to show for our efforts. If it hadn't been for that stupid skull, we'd at least have had our earnings from mudlarking. We were both feeling pretty fed up.

'P'raps we ought to try p-p-pinchin' the coppers' helmets next t-t-time.'

I didn't reply. Reg needed to get it out of his system.

'Very 'andy fer keepin' yer head d-d-dry when it's rainin'. What d-d-do you think, Jimmy?'

I kept quiet.

'Oh, 'ang about. Do you reckon we'd look a bit c-c-conspicuous? You know, me and you walkin' about Portsea in p-p-police helmets?'

I stopped him.

'All right, Reg. I'm sorry. Pinchin' the boots was a stupid idea. I'm sorry. Now can we forget it?'

Reg looked at me, smiled and then punched me a dead arm.

'F-f-forget what, Jimmy?'

We turned into Jubilee Terrace. Since the war, most of our neighbours had stuck Union Jacks up in their windows to show their support for the navy and Kitchener's army. Once one went up, it spread down the road, from neighbour to neighbour, like scabies. Mum said it was because people would think you weren't patriotic if you didn't.

Mum had started putting one up as a sign to me not to come in the house because she had company. We passed the alley and stopped outside my house. There was a flag up today.

We sat down on the kerb. The mud on our legs had dried and stiffened and was ready to be picked. We silently set to work, seeing who could get the biggest scab off. Reg had been thinking about the skull.

'I reckon 'e was a Hun saboteur who'd been caught in the act of blowin' up the Dockyard.'

I nodded. I was peeling off a giant chunk that was nearly four inches long. If I could manage it, it would be a world record. The wispy hairs on my leg were being pulled out one by one, but I didn't care.

'Yeah, he could have been secretly executed and dumped at sea.'

I held my breath. Nearly there. Two inches to go.

'And then been s-s-s-sliced up by a sh-sh-sh-ship's propellers,' added Reg with relish. He shut up when he saw how far I'd got.

'F-f-flippin' hell!'

One inch to go.

'That'll be the b-b-b-biggest . . .'

Suddenly, behind us, my front door slammed. The giant chunk turned to dust between my fingers.

We turned and glared at the bluejacket who was stooping down unsteadily to tie his boots. I could smell the booze on him from where we were sitting. The flag disappeared from the window.

Mum's friends always look a bit guilty and a lot drunk when they leave.

I guess it's another one of those laws of nature.

Reg patted me on the back, mumbled, 'See ya,' and crossed over to his house. He knew what it was like.

Don't get me wrong. I wasn't ashamed of me mum. She was the best.

But.

Chapter Four

The next day me and Reg went mudlarking as usual, but there was no sign of Archie and Lillie. I don't know whether the skull had spooked Archie, or whether he was just being protective of Lillie. Whichever, I didn't blame him.

Reg and I weren't going to let a skull interfere with business. Besides, the tide had come and gone twice, washing the slate clean. That's what I like about the sea. There's no messing about. No matter what has happened, it just gets on with it.

And that's what me and Reg tried to do. Except the slate wasn't clean and those crabs in my head were still pinching and twisting. I know it's stupid, but I was spooked too. I mean, we've all got skulls. But when we're dead they belong under the stone angels and crosses in St Thomas's churchyard, not staring up at you from the mud in Portsmouth Harbour.

Ah-ha! A Chief Petty Officer with a girl on each arm. He'd want to show how flush he is.

I cupped my hands and shouted up. 'Oy, chief! Bet you can't reach the water with a shillin'!'

Sure enough, he took up the challenge and threw his coin like he meant it. I could tell by its size and the way it flew that it was a tanner, not a shilling. The girls laughed as it dropped short of the water by a yard.

I could have beaten Reg to it, easy, but it landed in the mud where the skull had been, and I held back. I could have kicked myself. Silver in the morning was unheard of.

Reg did his party piece, a somersaulting dive, and held the coin up with a flourish. The girls cheered and clapped their appreciation and Reg delivered a formal, deep bow, which set them off laughing again. When they had gone he turned to me.

'What's up Jimmy? You could've g-g-got that one!'

'Dunno, Reg. I'm, er, I'm not, um, concentrating today.'

Reg bent down to wash the tanner in a rock pool, very pleased with himself. He looked up to the pier and followed the trajectory to where the coin had slipped into the mud.

'If he'd used a sh-sh-shilling, the extra weight would have carried it another five yards.'

I nodded. Five more yards and it would have been lost in twenty foot of water. No mudlark, not even a strong swimmer like Archie, would go out of his depth in the deadly currents of Portsmouth Harbour. Not for a shilling. Not even for a bag of gold sovereigns.

Perhaps it was the currents that had done for the German spy.

Or was it a suicide? A few weeks before, Jop told us that a mad woman had killed herself by filling her pockets with rocks and jumping off the end of the pier in the middle of the night. One of the Gosport boatmen had found her body the next morning when his anchor hooked her clothing, on the other side of the harbour. She'd been battered beyond recognition by the sea and the rocks. I'm glad we didn't find her.

'Do ya reckon the skull was a man or a woman's?'

Reg scratched his head, putting the muddy final touch to the only part of his body that wasn't black.

'D-d-dunno. A skull's a skull. How d'ya tell?'

I shrugged.

'Let's go and get a paper. It'll be in the morning edition.'

We made our way up to Jop's pitch on the pier. He was sitting on an upturned crate, with his arms folded and his eyes closed. A seagull was perched on his out-stretched wooden leg. Beside him was a tall, neat pile of the *Portsmouth Times*, with the top copy rippling in the breeze, barely anchored down by a few coins.

'Hello, Jop! How's business?'

The seagull took off and Jop opened his eyes, unfolded his arms and stood up to attention, his medals clanking against each other on his proud chest. Some white seagull shit dribbled off his wooden leg.

'Oh, 'ello, lads.'

'Having a n-n-nap, Jop?' Reg smiled as he asked the question. It was a game, and Reg knew which levers to pull.

'No, sir!' Jop boomed, scattering another dozen seagulls that had congregated on the pier railings behind him. 'Absolutely not. Sleeping on duty? Capital offence! No, sir! I was merely . . .' He looked out into the harbour until he found what he was looking for, 'I was merely . . . restin' me eyes.'

He shot us a wink and smiled.

'And I rested mine for eight hours last night!' I replied, enjoying the game. We all laughed, and Jop's medals danced a jig on his chest.

Jop's laughter turned into a wheezy cough and his medals began a new mad dance, which ended when he expertly gobbed a ball of phlegm into the air. Reg and I had seen this spectacle many times. If mudlarking is the eighth wonder, Jop's gobbing is a close ninth. We followed its progress as it arched over the pier decking. It hung in the air above the railway tracks, before falling smack bang between them, through the gap to the harbour mud below. That was one good reason why us mudlarks never went under the pier.

Another good reason was that the train toilets were emptied out there at the end of the long journey from Waterloo. You wouldn't believe how much sewage could come from a train full of soldiers. You wouldn't want that landing on the head of your worst enemy. Or perhaps you would.

'That did me good, lads,' Jop smiled in satisfaction, wiping his lips with his cuff. He adjusted his wooden leg and sat back down on his crate, exhausted.

'God blesses us all with one special gift. One special

talent. Mine just happens to be gobbin'. Now, can I sell you lads a paper?'

Reg stared at the huge pile of unsold papers.

'B–b–business a b–b–bit slow today?'

'You could say that without any fear of contradiction,' said Jop, shaking his head sadly. 'People was interested in the war when it started. But now? They're fed up with it! I've only sold two copies all morning. I reckon I'd make more money down in the mud with you lads.'

Reg and I looked down at Jop's wooden leg and exchanged a glance.

'All right, perhaps not,' Jop acknowledged with a chuckle. He was pretty agile, but not that agile.

Jop noticed the seagull poo on his wooden leg.

'That's a sure sign of good luck, lads. My fortune is about to change!'

I smiled and obliged.

'Can we double your sales and have a copy each?'

I rubbed the mud off two pennies, and Jop expertly folded and delivered the newspapers into the palms of our hands in a split second.

'Ta, lads.'

'We're looking to see who the skull in the mud belonged to. We reckon it could've been a German spy.'

Jop laughed and his medals threatened another knees–up.

'I never read the paper, so I couldn't tell you. Personally I don't believe a word they print, so even if they told me, I wouldn't know.'

I held my paper up, suppressing my smile.

'You mean this is full of lies? I want my money back!'

'Only jokin', lad. It's packed full of the absolute truth, and that comes with my personal guarantee. And my personal guarantee isn't worth the paper it isn't printed on.' While Reg and I tried to work that one out, Jop looked over the pier railings and mumbled under his breath, 'So that's what all that commotion was about yesterday.'

'Tarra, Jop, hope things pick up.'

'A nice juicy murder would do it!' laughed Jop. His voice trailed off as Reg and I walked towards the pier-head. 'There's nothing people like more than a nice, juicy murder!'

Reg and I sat down on the benches at Fog Corner, just outside the Dockyard Gate. Fog Corner was where dockies sat on the long benches and smoked their lungs out before the whistle went for their shift. Smoking in the Dockyard was a serious offence because of the risk of fire, so the benches were always packed just before the long shifts began. The hacking coughs and wheezing sounded pretty disgusting. People reckon that smoking is good for you because it purifies your lungs, but I have my doubts. Some of the things those dockies coughed up could have been bottled and sold as glue.

The place was ankle-deep in dog-ends, black pipe scrapings, dented tobacco tins, yellow gob and crushed Woodbine packets. Being barefoot meant you had to tread carefully, otherwise you could burn your soles on hot ash or smouldering fag-ends. Today we arrived mid-way between shifts, so it was safe. Even so, the place still stank of stale tobacco, stale smoke and stale sweat.

I turned the pages of the newspaper, scanning the columns, while Reg studied what was on at the picture house. While I'd picked up reading pretty quickly at school, Reg had struggled. He could usually make out the words, but it took a while. The teachers at Portsea Boys' thought he was an idiot because of his stammer and they ignored him, so he never learnt much.

'Ch-Ch-Charlie Ch-Ch-Chaplin's latest is on at the C-C-Coliseum.'

Reg put the paper down on the bench, satisfied that he had gleaned some useful information from it. He picked up a tin from the debris around his ankles and began collecting dog-ends. If you broke up about ten of them, you could collect enough tobacco for a decent smoke. Reg's ma loved a smoke but couldn't afford to, so Reg was always helping out that way.

When I was a kid I took some home for my mum, thinking she'd be pleased. But she went mad. Really mad. At the time I didn't understand why, but I think I do now. It was her pride. And I think she got all the cigarettes she wanted from her sailor and soldier customers.

I wondered if any of her customers were listed among the names of war casualties in the paper. It read,

HEROES WHO HAVE MADE THE ULTIMATE
SACRIFICE

There were about fifty names today, listed alphabetically, with their rank and name of ship or regiment.

Perhaps one of them, one of those names, one of those dead people, was my dad.

I kept thinking about my dad more and more. Who-ever he was, he kept getting into my head, uninvited. But he didn't have a face or a name.

I turned the page. Then, in the corner:

POLICE BOOTS STOLEN – GANG SOUGHT

'Hey, Reg. Look at this!' I read the article out aloud.

'Police are seeking a gang of thugs who, in an audacious raid yesterday, stole seven pairs of black leather police boots and police-issue socks valued at twenty-one pounds, seven shillings and seven pence. The culprits are believed to be aged around fifteen and are of dishevelled appearance. The stolen property was later recovered from a Portsea pawnbroker, but police fear that the gang could strike again. Chief Constable Thomas Lloyd said that since the war started there had been a dramatic increase in such crimes and that he attributed this to the absence of discipline, as many fathers were away fighting or engaged in war-work.'

It was a strange feeling. I know it's wrong, but I felt a little bit proud.

Reg looked up the article in his paper, pointing and

mouthing each word while I read it again to myself.

'What's d-d-dishevelled?'

'Means we're scruffy 'erberts.'

'B-b-bleedin' cheek. An' what's this about me an' you bein' a gang?'

'Dunno what they're playing at. I suppose it don't look so bad for them if they lost their boots to a gang rather than two fourteen-year-olds.'

'And all that s-s-stuff about d-d-dads and d-d-discipline,' Reg laughed, 'it's a load of old rubbish!'

'I know. That's one of the advantages of bein' a bustard! You got more freedom.'

Reg and I smiled at each other, mud brothers and bustards together.

I finished scanning the paper.

'That's really strange, that is. There's no mention of the skull anywhere!'

I flung the paper down in disgust. Reg looked up, incredulous. He squeezed the lid on his tin crammed full of dog-ends. It snapped shut.

'Why would they r-r-report a few old boots going missing, but not m-m-mention s-s-something like that?'

'Exactly,' I said. 'Something don't add up.'

Chapter Five

The Coliseum was packed that afternoon. Nobody wanted to miss the latest Charlie Chaplin. Reg and I got the worst of the morning's mud off with scrunched-up pages of our newspapers. If you turn up at the Coliseum too dirty, they make you stand at the back.

Reg used his tanner to get us in. The lady at the ticket office pulled a face because Reg hadn't done a very good job washing the coin.

'It's OK, m–m–missus,' explained Reg as he took the tickets. 'I just found it in a pile of fresh, s–s–steamin' 'orse dung.'

The lady's face turned to horror and she quickly dropped the coin into the till and tentatively sniffed her hand.

'That poor 'orse,' I said to Reg loudly as we walked away. 'Dire ear's a terrible thing.'

The Coliseum was called 'The Dream Palace', and not for no reason. Those moving pictures took you to places you'd never go, showed you things you'd never see and let you imagine you're people you'd never be. But they say that every silver lining has a cloud. There were two hidden menaces in the darkness of the Coliseum. Fleas that were after your blood. And perverts who were after something else. You got rid of the fleas by pressing a wet bar of carbolic soap on them when you got home. And you got rid of the perverts by shouting out loud at the top of your voice, 'Leave my willy alone, you dirty pervert bustard!'

Good old Charlie. There's something special about laughing your heart out with five hundred strangers in the dark. Good old Charlie brought us all together, made us feel part of something bigger. It's almost as special as crying your heart out with four thousand Pompey supporters at Fratton Park.

Reg and I didn't usually take any notice of the first film, but today it was called *The Enemy Within* and was about German spies. Reg and I settled back into our seats.

The pianist down at the front set the atmosphere with some deep, sinister chords. Spies are everywhere, listening for useful military and naval information and passing it back to the Kaiser in Berlin. They're disguised as shopkeepers, café owners, teachers, travelling salesmen. In fact, you couldn't be sure of anyone, because spies are trained to speak English exactly like you or me.

'Blimey! For all I know, you could be one, Reg,' I whispered.

Reg turned and, with a swift jab, gave me a dead arm.

'D-d-don't let on, will ya.'

The sinister chords turn into dramatic ones.

A black night. The moon hides behind dark clouds. A furtive, shadowy figure climbs a fence. He jumps down and hides behind a bush. An armed Tommy appears and the chords change from dramatic to patriotic. A notice tells us he is guarding the city reservoir. The man reaches the edge of the reservoir and laughs like a maniac to mad chords. A large bottle is pulled from the man's overcoat. We see the label.

A skull-and-crossbones and the words: DEADLY POISON.

The audience gasps. The mad, wide-eyed German goes to unstop the cork. The clouds move and reveal a full moon. The saboteur is illuminated by the moonlight. The soldier sees him, levels his rifle and takes aim.

A shot.

The saboteur falls. The cheers of the audience almost drown out the jubilant chords.

An old lady on the end of our row stood up and shook her umbrella at the screen. 'Serves 'im right, filthy Hun!'

A drunken soldier in the front row shouted, ''Ang the bleedin' Kaiser!'

The cheers were renewed.

A bluejacket shook his fist in anger. 'Hangin's too bleedin' good fer 'im!'

I cupped my hands and joined in. It was a laugh.

'Shoot 'em all!'

Another roar and more shouts, urging death to the

Germans and even nastier things for the Kaiser. The hate was infectious.

Reg looked at me, but didn't say anything.

Within a minute the reel had been changed and Charlie Chaplin appeared in his bowler hat, paint-brush moustache and swinging cane, waddling in that way that us mudlarks had studied, practised and perfected. The sight of Charlie instantly emptied the cinema of hate. And then, a moment later, Charlie had us cheering and laughing. Again and again. Waves of titters, chuckles, chortles and then belly laughs rolled up and down the rows until the whole place seemed to shake. The whole sea of silhouetted heads and shoulders was rocking and rolling like rowing boats down the harbour in a force nine.

The old bat at the end of our row was transformed back into a happy and harmless old lady, and the soldiers down the front were laughing like deep, deep drains. Reg and I had tears in our eyes, and they stayed there throughout the national anthem.

I leant over and whispered in Reg's ear. 'Never mind God saving the gracious bleedin' King, God save good old Charlie!'

I had to whisper. Rumour was that people got hung for less.

'G-g-good old Charlie!' repeated Reg, as we shuffled out and blinked in the daylight.

'Yeah.' I shook my head but meant more than yes. 'Good old Charlie!'

★

'F-f-fancy a toffee apple round Archie's?'

Now, this was a long tradition. After going to the cinema we always had a Vosbrugh's toffee apple if we could afford it.

'Yeah. Why not?'

I tried to scratch the middle of my back.

Reg helped me out. 'You got c-c-caught again, then?'

'Yeah. And all over me legs. It's a law of nature. There's somethin' about me they can't bleedin' resist. Must be the royal blood in me veins, on account of me dad. Fleas like somethin' that's a bit more refined than the common stuff sloshin' around in your body.'

Reg rarely got bitten, and I had a theory.

But so did Reg. 'Nah. It's the the refined s-s-stuff like m-m-mine they keeps fer s-s-special occasions.'

Mrs Vosbrugh's sweetshop window had to be cleaned every day because of the smears and smudges made by the hundreds of snotty, salivating Portsea kids who pressed their faces against it. The bay window enabled you to study the day's offerings from different angles. It was packed with trays of creamy toffees, soft or brittle, mixed with raisins or peanuts, crumbly slabs of fudge, bars of thick, milky chocolate, chunks of cherry nougat and individual chocolates, handmade and stuffed with goodies by Mr Vosbrugh. In the middle were the freshly made toffee apples, sticks uppermost and stuck to the tray by glistening, treacly toffee.

Reg and I had grown out of pressing our faces against the window, but we couldn't let go of those toffee apples.

They were made by Mr Vosbrugh at the back of the shop, and the smell of the toffee wafting out from Alfred Street into Queen's Street drew kids from the nearby terraced streets far better than the school bell ever did.

We'd grown up with the smell of toffee, caramel and fudge, and we still found them irresistible.

The doorbell tinkled as we entered. Mr Vosbrugh was crouched over a tray of dark chocolates with an icing bag. He deftly waved the nozzle in a way that reminded me of Jop's folding of newspapers, an effortless skill that takes years to master.

Mr Vosbrugh was a huge, powerful man, and it was always funny to see him concentrating all his efforts on delicate confectionery. His huge hands squeezed the bag and directed the nozzle with precision, leaving behind an identical white iced squiggle on each chocolate.

Mrs Vosbrugh smiled.

'Welcome, Jimmy and Reggy! You have been to the cinema, no?'

'Yes, Mrs Vosbrugh, the latest Charlie Chaplin is showing at the Coliseum. It was great, you must see it!'

A flea moved and I scratched my leg.

'Yes, he is our favourite too, is he not, Hercule?'

Mr Vosbrugh grunted and stood back from the tray, surveying his squiggles with satisfaction.

Reg peered over the counter.

'I haven't seen that t-t-type before. Is it a new range?'

'Yes, Hercule is trying out the rum flavour. The sailors, they like the rum, no?'

Reg nodded. Mr Vosbrugh was always trying to think of ways to increase his business. He was a man of few words but many ideas. One of his enterprises was selling postcards of naked French ladies to sailors and soldiers or anyone else who had a shilling. It was illegal and top secret, of course, but everyone knew about it, except for Mrs Vosbrugh, so we were under strict instructions never to mention it in the shop. Mr Vosbrugh employed Sam the Telegram to distribute them around Portsea on his Post Office bicycle.

Let me tell you about Sam. He was in the same class as us at Portsea Boys' and had been covered in spots for as long as I can remember. When he left school, he became a telegram boy because of the boots. Post Office boots were quality. Everyone eyed them up with envy. Brown leather, twelve-hole, hand-stitched. Fortunately the job required him to also wear a dodgy uniform and a silly peaked cap, so everyone could take the piss out of him and hide their envy. By everyone I mean, of course, me and Reg.

Sam pocketed a penny commission on each postcard, and he made so much money that he didn't really need his Post Office wages. But his uniform was a good cover – not that he needed one, because most of the local coppers were good customers.

Thanks to Sam the Telegram, Reg and I had an impressive collection of Paris ladies under our beds. We regularly had swapping sessions, though there were some cards I would never swap. I kept them tucked safely beneath a loose floorboard under the join in the lino, which I covered up with my chamber pot.

Mrs Vosbrugh pointed towards the window display.

'The usual? Or can I tempt you with something else? Today, the nougat, it is so chewy you can stretch it for a foot before it snaps!'

'No, the usual, please. Five toffee apples.'

'B-b-biggest on the tray,' added Reg.

Mrs Vosbrugh winked. 'That, it goes without saying!'

Chapter Six

'That's a daft way of counting the paving stones, Arch!'

Archie was on his knees, chalking out numbers on the pavement outside his house in Barrack Street. Lillie was sitting on the doorstep, clutching her rag-doll and watching intently.

Archie looked up, annoyed and embarrassed. 'I'm teaching Lillie how to play hopscotch, you idiot.'

'You're so easy to wind up, Arch!' I held up the toffee apples. 'Now, who wants one who doesn't think I'm an idiot?'

'Lillie don't fink you're an idot,' said Lillie without taking her eye off the toffee apples. She held up rag-doll-Lillie. 'And Lillie don't neivver.'

I handed two to Lillie and gave Reg his, but held back on Archie's until he agreed that I wasn't an idiot.

'Thanks, you idiot,' Archie laughed as he took it and Reg and I sat down next to him. We didn't say another word as we bit into the cracking toffee and crisp, juicy apple. Lillie pushed one into rag-doll-Lillie's face and took a lick of the other, then took it in turns.

'We's sharin',' Lillie explained to rag-doll-Lillie.

'That went down a treat!' said Archie as we all finished together, 'Ready? Go!'

In one movement we threw our sticks, top-heavy with the impaled cores, into the gutter on the other side of the road, like hand grenades into an enemy trench, flinging ourselves flat on to the pavement, shouting, 'Kabooooom!'

While we were flat, avoiding the flying shrapnel, Archie asked, 'What happened about the skull? Who was it?'

'Fraid we d-d-don't know,' explained Reg. 'There ain't been n-n-nothing in the newspaper.'

'There was a bit about us though,' I added. I got the article out of my pocket, unfolded it and handed it to him.

Archie sat up and read it, laughing at the bit about the gang.

''S funny they don't mention the skull. It's not something the sea chucks up every day.'

'Nah. Me and Reg reckons it could've been a German spy or saboteur, trying to get ashore from a U-boat in the Channel, and they're keepin' quiet about it.'

'Likely got s-s-sliced up by a sh-sh-ship's propellers,' explained Reg. He seemed to like his idea a bit too much.

'Yeah, I've 'eard that they're everywhere, these Hun spies . . .'

'I spoys with moy little oy . . .'

Lillie was looking all around for something to spoy, her mouth crammed with toffee.

Archie replied, 'Something beginning with B,' and smiled at his sis before returning to the conversation.

'Yeah, they're everywhere. Portsmouth's swarming with 'em. My dad said that some are disguised as barbers. They chat up their customers, get naval and military secrets, and then slit their throats from ear to ear.' Archie motioned a line across his throat, pulling a grotesque face. 'And there are others that sell poisoned cigarettes and food to soldiers and sailors.'

'Bustards,' I breathed angrily. Archie was confirming what we'd seen in that film.

'Bustards!' shouted Lillie through her mouthful, enjoying the new word almost as much as the toffee. She held out her two toffee apples to Reg and me, minus the toffee. She had licked both apples clean, and they were glistening with spit.

'Dese is for you.'

The flag was down. Mum didn't have company. I smiled. It meant she wouldn't be smelling of gin.

'If it ain't muddy mud, it's flippin' fleas! I don't know! Look at yer legs!'

I looked at my legs.

'Yer a bleedin' 'uman pincushion again!'

I agreed.

'Well, don't just stand there! They'll 'ave all yer blood! And then where would yer be?'

I thought about that one.

'Empty?'

Mum smiled. She pulled the tin bath off the wall and dropped it on to the cobbles.

'Well, I hope your flamin' Charlie Chaplin film was worth it.'

'It was, Mum.'

'Give us yer clothes an' I'll boil 'em up.'

She handed me a wet, squidgy bar of carbolic. I began pressing it on the tiny specks that flecked my legs and waist while Mum filled up the tub with steaming water.

'Do you reckon fleas go 'ome to the big ma flea covered in blood, the way you comes home to yours covered in mud?' she laughed.

'These won't,' I replied, proudly showing her the nine flea corpses embedded in the soap.

After my bath I felt cleaner than clean. Fleas can really bug you if you don't sort them out. They make you feel really dirty in a way that all the mud in the world couldn't. And people start calling you a fleabag. There are some names that you can live with, and there are some names that you can't.

Mum served up my favourite supper, roast chicken leg with roast potatoes, and we sat and ate it together at the kitchen table. We always kept that sharp bone you find in the middle to pick the skin out of our teeth afterwards. It was one of our little ceremonies. I loved it when she had an evening off. Those were our evenings.

I thought about the names that Mum lived with.

Because of her way of life. Because of her drinking. I remember when I didn't know what they meant. They were just words that you overheard.

I knew now.

And they were names far worse than fleabag.

I wanted to talk to her. I wanted her to stop the pub work, stop her drinking, so that those names could not be true.

But I didn't want to spoil our evening.

I didn't want to spoil anything.

I told her all about how we'd found the skull, but I left out the bit about the boots. Mum wouldn't have approved of that. She looked horrified when I mentioned the skull, but she said we'd done the right thing by not getting involved with the police.

Looking back, I could tell there was something wrong. Something about that skull had spooked her. I didn't know whether it was the skull itself, or the fact that I was involved in finding it. Perhaps she could tell it had spooked me more than I let on. I tried to find out.

'Mum, what's up?'

She seemed distracted.

'Oh, oh nothing, Jimmy.'

'But you're very quiet, Mum. You sure there's nothing wrong?'

'Just a bit tired. Nuffin' to worry about. Eat up. I've got a special treat fer yer afters.'

Mum got up and fetched my treat from the larder. It was a toffee apple from Vosbrugh's.

'Thanks, Mum!'

Two in one day! It's funny, but that toffee apple tasted better than any I'd ever had before. The toffee seemed thicker and creamier. As I bit into it, the glaze cracked like the ice on a frozen pond, revealing the crisp, white, succulent apple.

I savoured every single bite. And after every bite I savoured every mouthful and, after every mouthful, every swallow. Finally, I licked away the last fragments of toffee from my lips and realized that something was changing. I knew I would have to talk to her. I couldn't keep just thinking about it. I had to really do it.

But how to say what I wanted to say?

Chapter Seven

Sunday. Some people go to church. God knows why.

Don't get me wrong. That's up to them. That's their choice. But for us mudlarks Sundays always promised to be a good day, but the church was in competition with us. The thing was, the vicar was trying to get his hands on coins that were rightfully ours.

'I don't g-g-get it,' said Reg, 'The vicar 'as a go at everybody for d-d-doin' stuff they shouldn't do, and then passes a plate round askin' for their d-d-dosh!'

'Unbelievable,' I agreed. 'I might be missing something, but it is my personal opinion that we give far better value for money.'

Sunday – the day of rest. You can't beat it. People are relaxed, carefree, more likely to part with their small change. You can see it in their faces. The sun has come out and they are smiling. You can't go far wrong on a sunny Sunday. Days like today almost made you think that God must be a really good bloke.

★

The churches must be empty. Hundreds of people have come down the harbour.

Reg and I could sense the coins bouncing and jangling in their pockets and purses. We had this theory that they were desperately trying to break free and escape to their rightful home in our pockets. And that it just took a little bit of our natural magnetism to make it happen.

On Sundays, Reg and I sometimes say, 'Bless you,' to the punters when we've retrieved their coin. It's a nice touch and goes down really well, especially with old people. Us mudlarks have a reputation for bringing good luck, a bit like chimney sweeps, four-leaf clover, or touching a sailor's collar. Don't get me wrong. I'm not claiming our blessings have the same clout as the vicar's, but they're appreciated just the same.

A group of girls was walking arm-in-arm up the pier, singing and laughing. I spotted them first. Aged about sixteen. Maybe older. Game for a laugh. No blessings needed here.

'Oy, ladies! See the full moon fer a tanner!'

I bent over, turned and wiggled at them.

They looked down over the railing at us, whispering to each other behind their hands and giggling. The girl in the middle smiled at me and I smiled back. She blinked and I noticed her eyes. Immediately I wished I hadn't offered a full moon. I felt like a stupid, naughty little boy.

She snapped open her purse and a coin spun down. She might have nice eyes, but she couldn't throw to save her life.

Reg and I did the business, diving to the spot where it landed. I tried harder than usual. I beat him, no problem, and held up a thruppenny coin with a flourish. Then I bowed deeply to the girl in the middle like a knight honouring his lady.

'Where's my full moon, then?' she smiled, raising her eyebrows expectantly. If she didn't have such nice eyes and smile, I'd have thought she was making fun of me. The other girls laughed and egged her on.

'I said a full moon fer a tanner. This,' I held up her coin, 'is a thruppenny piece.'

I knew immediately I said it. She was quick.

'Maths isn't my strong point, but isn't that worth a half-moon?' The girls giggled and leant far over the railings to get a good look. She had me, and everyone knew it. Normally I wouldn't have cared. What does it matter who sees my arse? It's in the repertoire. We'd all done it a hundred times. It always got a laugh.

One of the girls pulled out a pair of those binoculars you use at the music hall when you're stuck at the back. She focused them on me. I really didn't want to do this. But I knew I didn't have a choice.

The girl with the nice eyes put her chin on her hand and tilted her head. 'Fancy a date instead?'

Her friends groaned in disappointment and laughed and pushed her and told her she was awful.

Reg looked at me in disbelief.

'Yeah, great!' I said, my surprise hiding my relief.

She thought for a second.

'How about the fifth of July, eighteen ninety-eight?'

The girls collapsed into laughter. She had me again. I liked her, so I pushed it, risked it.

'Fancy tea at the Swiss Caff?'

'Who's paying?'

I held up her thruppenny piece.

'You are!'

'It'll cost you more than that to take me out!'

'How 'bout next Sunday?'

She smiled. 'Next Sunday's fine by me.'

'Six?'

'I don't finish at the factory until six. We've got overtime, stitching army kitbags. How 'bout seven?'

'Seven's fine by me.'

We stared at each other for a few seconds. She had a blue bonnet on, and wisps of light brown curly hair framed her face.

'What's your name?'

'Madelaine. But my friends call me . . .'

'Mad!' chorused the other girls, bursting into laughter. Madelaine looked at them with mock disapproval and smiled.

'I'm Maddy. My friends call me Maddy.'

'Nice to meet you, Maddy. I'm Jimmy.'

She nodded and smiled again and looked at me intently.

'Don't worry,' I reassured her, pointing to my mud-encrusted clothes, 'this is me working gear.'

The girls giggled.

'I'll make an effort fer our date, just fer you, Maddy.'

'Well I'm honoured, kind sir. And I shall show my

appreciation by wearing the best dress in my wardrobe.'

Her friends cooed soppily and then laughed, but Maddy could take it.

'See ya, Maddy.'

'See ya, then, Jimmy.'

Maddy and her friends skipped off, arm in arm, laughing, the planks of the pier shaking noisily. I held her thruppenny piece tightly in my fist.

'Blimey, Jimmy. How d-d-did you do that?' Reg still looked a bit stunned by my eagerness to retrieve that particular coin, and at my prize.

'Dunno. Either you've got it . . .' I looked Reg up and down, 'or you 'aven't.'

We laughed.

'She's very, um, p-p-pretty.' Reg mumbled the word like he'd never come across it before.

'Yeah,' I smiled. 'I noticed that.'

'You smug git. G-G-God knows what she s-s-sees in you.'

I scooped up a handful of mud and slung it. Reg ducked and in one smooth movement returned a ball that glanced off the side of my head, filling my left ear with mud and knocking me over.

'Blimey, Jimmy, you should've d-d-dodged that one. Or has true l-l-love knackered yer reflexes?'

I held out my hand and Reg came over to pull me out. He should have expected the yank on his arm, and I think he did. He lost his balance and splatted and sank into the mud beside me, and we laughed together as we

63

stared up at the sky. Mud brothers. Nothing could change that.

That night, while sitting in the bath in the backyard, I washed the mud off Maddy's thruppenny piece and rinsed it clean. I've kept it on me ever since, and I have it in my hand right now, as I wait.

Chapter Eight

Queen's Street Police Station was a grim place. It smelt of disinfectant, as if the police had been trying to kill crime with it. But the smell of sick and piss hung around defiantly. I didn't want to be here. Reg didn't want to be here either, but I talked him into it. It took a bit of doing, but, once I'd convinced him that nobody would recognize us as the Boot Gang, he reluctantly agreed. As long as I did all the talking.

It was over a week since we'd found the skull and I couldn't stand the not knowing, and neither could Reg. We'd kept Jop happy, buying a paper every day. But still nothing. Jop said that while he appreciated the business, we should stop worrying about it. There was probably a reasonable explanation. If it was a spy, the authorities might want to hush it up.

And Jop said that if it was a suicide, there'd been so many since the war that they probably didn't bother reporting them any more. They needed the room to list all the war casualties.

Whatever had happened, I wanted to know. I felt sort of responsible for finding out, for understanding.

'Good morning, officer.'

I liked that. It sounded respectful, but not too cosy. But Reg looked at me as if I'd just licked the policeman's arse. The owner of the arse was behind a high desk like a pedestal and all that I could see of him was his head. He didn't say anything or look up. Over his shoulder, on the wall, was a framed picture of the King with lots of medals. I wasn't impressed. As far as I knew, King George hadn't fought in any wars like Jop, so I wondered how he'd got them all.

The policeman was writing. Every time he stopped scratching with his nib I thought he'd look up, but then we heard him dip his pen in his inkpot and the scratching resumed.

I realized how the King had got his medals. He must have awarded them to himself. You can get away with murder when you're a king. I wondered if he had a ceremony, where he pinned them on his own chest. 'Well done, me,' he would say to himself as he slapped himself on his own back.

Reg and I coughed and shuffled our feet for several minutes. It was our way of saying 'We're here'. The scratching of the pen was the policeman's way of saying that he didn't care. At long last his pen stabbed a full stop and he peered down at us through a pair of reading glasses.

'What do you want?'

I couldn't tell whether he was standing or sitting. If he was standing, he'd be seven foot tall. If he was sitting down, he'd be nine. But then I realized that he must be on some sort of raised platform. Either that or he'd escaped from Berty Bertram's Circus of Oddities.

'We were wonderin' if you could tell us anything about the skull that was found in the mud in the 'arbour last week.'

The constable pulled off his glasses and looked down at us intently.

'And what skull might that be?'

'We just 'appened to be around when some kid found this skull. In the mud. In the 'arbour.'

'And what might you know about it?'

'Like I say, nothing. We just 'appened to be there at the time. Just passin', like, as you do, mindin' our own business. There was five blasts on a whistle and more policemen arrived.'

The mention of five blasts seemed to alarm him. He leant forward, towering over us, his brow furrowed and his finger pointing.

'What . . . what do you know about the whistle code?'

'Well, nothing, really. We just wondered . . .'

'Why are you interested in the number of whistles?'

'We, er, we're not. It's just that we'd never heard that number before.'

I shrugged as innocently as I could, but I realized I'd

given away more than I should. I had acknowledged the existence of the whistle code, and now he knew that we knew more than we should. That made me feel guilty of something terrible, so I tried even harder to seem innocent. He frowned down at us, sizing and weighing us up.

After a long silence he licked his lips. 'Do you know what curiosity did to the cat?'

I was starting to realize that Reg had been right. This was a bad idea. A big mistake.

'I'll enlighten you. Curiosity did *for* the cat. Understood?'

Reg and I nodded our understanding, even though we didn't.

'So forget about skulls. Forget about whistle codes. And remember. We can have you bustards any time we want. Loitering. Begging. Breathing. Existing. We can have you any time we like. Any time we think you're becoming . . . a problem.'

We understood that bit.

The glasses reappeared on his head and he went back to his scratching. Reg and I left the station like cats out of hell.

We didn't stop till we reached the Hard. The Dockyard was about to start a shift, so we felt anonymous and safe in the crowd of dockies who were hanging around Fog Corner, waiting for the whistle to go. I bent down to put my hands on my knees and get my breath back.

'Was he threatenin' us?'

'I think that's a r-r-reasonable interpretation,' gasped

Reg. 'You know, sometimes, Jimmy, you take the b-b-bleedin' b-b-biscuit. Oh, let's ask the nice b-b-bleedin' policeman. You b-b-bleedin' prat!'

Reg punched me a dead arm, but I didn't retaliate. He was right. I'd forgotten one of the basic laws of nature. All coppers are bustards.

'I'm sorry, Reg. But at least we know fer a fact that somethin' is going on.'

'Well p-p-personally I can live without knowin' what's g-g-goin' on, if it's all the same to you.'

The Dockyard whistle blasted, making us both jump. We burst out laughing as if it was funniest thing in the world. Tired dockies scowled and put out their pipes and cigarettes. There was nothing funny about a sixteen-hour shift.

Chapter Nine

Sunday. Soaking in the tub in the backyard.

Mum was indoors, mopping the kitchen floor. I could hear the slop and drag of the mop.

She shouted to me. 'What's the matter, Jimmy? It's not like you to spend so long in the tub!'

Mum was right. She doesn't miss much.

'No. I'm goin' out tonight. Just want to make sure all the mud's out of my hair.'

Mum poked her head round the back door.

'Oh yeah,' she winked. 'Goin' somewhere nice? I hear the King's in town today. Is that why you're gettin' all poshed up? You after a knighthood?'

She must have noticed that I'd got my best shirt and trousers out, the ones I don't wear when I'm mudlarking.

'Yeah, that's right, Mum. You'd 'ave to call me sir and wait on me, 'and an' foot.'

Mum folded her arms. 'No difference there, then.'

I laughed. 'Naah, Mum. I'm just off to the Swiss Caff. So I won't be wanting tea, thanks.'

'Very well, Sir James,' said Mum, pretending to be

upset. 'If my food's not good enough fer yer lordship . . .'

'That's right, Mum,' I agreed. 'I've waited fourteen years to tell you. Now you know.'

I sat at the table while Mum spread some dripping on her toast. Sunday was Mum's night with Poll. Poll was one of the sisters. That was what they were called, the women in Mum's circle. So when I talk about Mum's sisters, I'm not talking about my aunties. Every Sunday, Mum and Poll got poshed up and went to the King's Crown in Southsea, well away from all the soldiers and sailors.

'You out with Poll tonight, Mum?'

Mum swallowed a mouthful of toast.

'No. I 'aven't a clue where Poll is. I ain't seen her for over two months. The first couple of weeks I turned up at the Crown as usual, but she just didn't show up. And she ain't been working in her usual pubs.'

I could tell she was worried, but she did her best to hide it.

'Like as not she's gone off with some bluejacket to spend his life savings! That's just the sort of thing Poll would do!'

She laughed. Her friends in the business did it all the time. They always came back when the money ran out, but it didn't usually take two months.

'P'rhaps she's struck lucky and found someone with a bundle of money. You should never look a gift horse in the mouth.'

But she didn't sound convinced, and the worried look returned.

'If you see her round town, Jimmy, can you ask her to get in touch? Just to put me mind at rest.'

'Course, Mum.'

But I wasn't really thinking about Mum, or Poll, or gift horses. I didn't think about the skull either. I was thinking about Maddy.

I spat into my hand and sleeked back my hair in Albertolli's Swiss Caff window. I could see the reflection of the Town Hall clock over my shoulder. Five to seven. I smiled at how flippin' handsome I was, checked my flies, rattled the money in my pocket, and went in.

Albertolli's was not the poshest of posh, just posh. It had flowers in vases and brilliant white tablecloths. I didn't feel comfortable going in there. Customers' eyes darted down to my bare feet and they whispered across their tables. Mr Albertolli was all right, though. He treated me the same as anyone else, once I showed him that I had some cash.

The first pot of tea brought by Mr Albertolli lasted me forty minutes.

How long do you wait before you accept the fact? Are there rules somewhere that tell you?

There were three and a half cups in the pot. And no sign of Maddy. I'll give her five minutes. Then another five. Then another . . .

A late bus? The timetables had probably all gone to pot, what with the King's visit.

★

There are some nice-looking pastries with cherries and nuts at the counter. I should feel hungry, but I don't fancy anything.

Perhaps her tram had jumped its track?

The second pot arrives. Mr Albertolli raises an eyebrow, smiles and says I must be very thirsty.

Perhaps she had to work late at the factory? Overtime on a Sunday was probably worth it.

No. I must be mad. Seven cups of tea, and it's ten past eight. I've been stood up. No doubt about it. Or perhaps she misheard and went to the wrong caff? Well, it's possible.

Mr Albertolli only charged me for one pot. He knew that I'd been stood up. I knew it too. I tried to leave with dignity, but I felt that everyone in the caff was laughing at me behind their menus. Mr Albertolli wished me a good evening as he closed the door behind me. I caught my reflection in the window and realized how pug-ugly I was.

'W-w-well?'

'Well what, Reg?'

'Wh-wh-what 'appened?'

Reg shut his front door behind him and we started walking down to the harbour. Nobody likes Monday mornings, and I especially didn't like this one.

'Mind yer own bleedin' business.'

'She b-b-blew you out, then?'

I nodded. 'Yeah. Made me look a right Charlie.'

'That's b-b-bad. I could've s-s-sworn she really f-f-fancied you.'

'Yeah, me too.' I remembered the way she looked at me and smiled. 'Perhaps it's cos I'm a mudlark. Perhaps if I 'ad a proper job. And a pair of boots . . . Perhaps she saw me sittin' there in the Swiss Caff with nothin' on my feet and ran away.'

'You're t-t-talkin' crap, Jimmy. If anyone don't like ya cos of the way you are, that's their p-p-problem. That's what you always t-t-tell me when people take the p-p-piss out of my s-s-stammer.'

We turned the corner of Queen's Street and looked down at the Hard and the harbour.

I put my arm round Reg's shoulder. 'You're right, Reg. Thanks. Now let's forget girls. Who needs 'em? Let's go and do some mudlarking!'

We sprinted down into the mud, shouting at the tops of our voices like we were about to attack an enemy. The seagulls took off, alarmed, and we waded out to our favourite spot in the mud. Archie was already there, waiting for us.

But something was wrong. Lillie wasn't with him, and he looked deadly serious.

Chapter Ten

Archie pointed at me accusingly.

'We had the coppers round our 'ouse last night, cos of you!'

'What? What are you talking about, Archie?'

'They were looking for the Boot Gang.'

'But . . . what do you mean? . . . Why would they? . . .'

'The socks, you idiots! You left a trail of smelly socks all the way to my back gate! They brought a dog in special – not that they needed it with the way they stunk!'

Reg and me looked at each other. I knew that he was asking himself the same question. Archie wouldn't rat on us, would he?

Archie's anger gave way to worry.

'Look. They reckon I'm a member of the gang. And they're not gonna give up. You made them look stupid, and they want you bad. They took our 'ouse apart, lookin' fer evidence.'

I glanced at Reg again, and then back at Archie.

'You didn't mention us, did you, Archie?'

'Course not. But they keep comin' back to our 'ouse. Me ma is livid. She thinks I'm involved too.'

'But why would she think that?'

'Lillie told her. It wasn't her fault. Now Ma says I can't be trusted to look after her.' His anger returned, 'And it's all your fault!'

'C-c-come on, Archie. They've g-g-got no evidence.'

'But they know . . .'

'They know nothing. Nothing at all. They're tryin' it on. That's what they do.'

'But . . .'

'They can't t-t-touch you,' Reg added, patting him on the back reassuringly.

Archie put his hands on his head and ruffled his hair, as if this would help him think more clearly.

'I s'pose . . . I s'pose you're right.'

'Anyway, Archie, the coppers will be too busy investigating the skull we found to spend much time on a few old boots.'

'Yeah, you're right.'

It was an excellent day for mudlarking. The sun was out and the rumble of trains arriving at the station packed with soldiers was non-stop. By midday I'd made nearly three shillings and I reckon Reg and Archie had about the same. We'd put the boot business behind us and were having a great time. There were some other lads mudlarking, but we didn't mind because there was enough trade to go round. When the Dockyard whistle blew at one, Archie went home for dinner while Reg and I went up on the pier.

★

Jop was explaining to a Royal Artillery officer what we were doing wrong in the war.

'In them days we had horses and swords and lances. None of this trying to kill the enemy without getting within a mile of 'em! Where's the glory in that? Nobody wants to read about it.'

The soldier explained that he wanted a newspaper, not a history lesson, so Jop took his money and delivered one into his hand without another word.

'Hello, lads!'

He waited until the soldier was out of earshot.

'The customer is always right, even when he's wrong, eh, lads? What do you think?'

Reg and I looked at each other.

'What about, Jop?'

'The war, lads, the war!'

'Well, it's been good for us. We earn almost three times as much mudlarkin' with all these bluejackets and Tommies around. Today's been great.'

I showed him my two handfuls of muddy coins.

Jop nodded, but he had reservations. 'This can't go on forever. Lots of 'em are going away and not coming back. One of the first rules of business is to maintain customer loyalty. And goin' away to get killed might be loyal to yer King and country, but it ain't flippin' well loyal to me. Old Lord Kitchener don't consider that.'

Reg and I laughed.

'Talkin' of customer loyalty . . .' Jop folded a paper and took a penny, 'I hope you'll keep readin' the paper, now your mystery has been solved. Have a look at page four.'

'I thought you said you never r-r-read the p-p-paper!'

Reg had caught him out.

'I don't.' He coughed dishonestly. 'I merely scans it on occasion.'

I found the article at the bottom of the page in the last column.

'Harbour Suicide.'

My heart sank. I started reading it out for Reg's benefit.

'The City Coroner has established that the skull found washed up at Portsea Hard is that of a woman of ...' I thought about Mum and swallowed hard, 'a woman of known disreputable and drunken habits. Polly Grant, aged twenty-three, is believed to have committed suicide several months ago by jumping off the Railway Pier.'

Was it Poll? I didn't know her surname, none of the sisters ever used them. Nobody ever called her Polly, though. She was Poll. One of the sisters? Mum's friend? I didn't say anything. I didn't know. I was thinking of Mum.

Jop looked over the pier railings, shaking his head sadly. Overhead, some seagulls hung in the sea breeze, crying.

Reg looked disappointed. 'You m-m-mean it w-w-wasn't a German s-s-spy?'

I ignored Reg and carried on reading. 'Recording a verdict of "suicide while the balance of her mind was disturbed", the Coroner indicated that tidal action and strong currents had dismembered the body and sea creatures had done the rest. More remains and clothes were found up-harbour near Portchester Castle. No relatives have been traced and her remains will be interred in a pauper's grave at Milton Cemetery next week.'

Reg was shaking his head. 'N-n-no. That can't be it. There m-m-must be m-m-more to it than that!'

All sorts of things were going through my mind. Mum. Poll. Those hungry crabs. The skull. The policeman, staring and threatening.

Reg was right. Something didn't add up.

'This Polly Grant. I think she might be one of my mum's friends. Poll. One of the sisters. Mum thought she'd run off with a sailor.'

Jop looked me in the eyes.

'I'm very sorry to hear about that, lad, if it is her.'

'There's something wrong here, Jop. Why should the police try to warn us off?'

A bluejacket was relieved of his penny and provided with a neatly rolled newspaper.

'I shouldn't worry about it, lads. It's probably nothin'. And with due respect, Jimmy, perhaps the police just thought it was none of yer business. And if there is more to it than meets the eye, you can't do nothing about it. That's something you learns in the army. Keep yer 'ead down.'

'P'rhaps,' I said, unconvinced. 'What really got the copper goin' was when I mentioned the whistle code.'

Jop cleared his throat as if to say something, but brought up some phlegm. He thought for a second and then, out of respect, swallowed it. If the harbour was poor Poll's grave − or anyone else's for that matter − he didn't want to do the unforgivable.

'There's a motto that's stood me in good stead all me life. In fact, it's probably why I'm still on God's earth rather than in it . . .'

Reg and I exchanged a glance. We really didn't want Jop's advice.

'Never trouble trouble till trouble troubles you.'

Jop left a silence for us to absorb his wisdom. Reg looked at Jop's chest and then down at his wooden leg.

'And that's how you w-w-won all them m-m-medals and lost yer leg, was it, Jop?'

Jop smiled. Overhead, some seagulls hung in the sea breeze, laughing.

'Point taken, lad. Point taken.'

But then the smile left his face and he suddenly looked grave. I saw something in his eyes that I'd never seen before.

Worry.

I think he noticed me see that worry, and he looked away to hide it. The seagulls were motionless, like they were pinned to the clouds, and their laughs became cries became screams as the wind cranked up to a force five.

'Seriously, lads. My advice is to leave it alone. Remember, don't trouble trouble : . .'

Reg and I sat on the kerb, picking at the dried mud. A large chunk on my calf looked promising but cracked into two at the last minute. Reg's best effort also crumbled.

The flag was up and, as usual, Reg was keeping me company until it came down and I could go in for my bath and supper.

'Fancy a game of I Spy?'

'Very b–b–bleedin' funny.' Reg was disappointed that his theory of a Hun saboteur being sliced up by a ship's propellers had been knocked on the head.

'That's a "no" then, is it?'

The lamppost on the corner outside the Nelson pub flickered on and curtains began to be drawn along the terrace as people decided they'd had enough of the day. Every time the pub door opened we'd hear a few notes of squeeze box before it sprang shut again. Reg and I tried a game of naming the songs but then gave up. We figured that the bloke squeezing the squeeze box was so drunk we wouldn't recognize any of them even if the door was wedged wide open permanently.

The Nelson was popular with bluejackets, and Mum and her sisters got a lot of work there, serving and collecting glasses. You'd think that everyone would be in competition for the work, but it wasn't like that. They always let each other know if they heard of any jobs going, and at chucking-out time they all looked out for each other as if they were real sisters. The streets could be dangerous for women on their own after dark.

Rumour had it that aristocrats and even royalty came down in disguise to slum it in the Portsea pubs, but the sisters never broke their code of silence, so it stayed a rumour. It didn't stop Reg and me speculating from time to time.

'Course, you kn-kn-know that P-P-Prince Albert 'as got a b-b-bit of a st-st-stutter.'

'Yeah. I'd 'eard that, Reg. Several times. Now who was it who told me? Oh, yes. You did, Reg.'

'It's a fact,' asserted Reg, stretching his neck in a regal manner.

Then we laughed. We knew we were just a couple of little bustards really, cos that's what people called us. But it was fun thinking about it. Being a prince. Being an heir to the throne. And, secretly, you can wish whatever you like. Nobody can mess with your wishes, however daft they might be.

'We c-c-could even be 'alf-bruvvers. P-P-Prince Reginald and P-P-Prince James.'

I shook my head, 'Yeah. That's likely.'

But I liked the idea. Me and Reg half-brothers. I repeated the names slowly in my very best posh.

'Prince Reginald and Prince James. Naah. Prince Reginald don't sound right.'

Reg had to agree, so I inherited the title.

Prince James. I could pin medals on my own chest, like the King. And I'd have the best pair of boots money could buy. Twelve hole, finest leather, made by the most skilled cobbler in the land.

The squeeze box stopped suddenly and three sisters stumbled out of the Nelson, arm in arm with three blue-jackets and screaming with laughter. Two more sisters followed and danced off towards Queen's Street, probably to try their luck in the soldiers' pub, the Artillery Arms.

Reg and I finished picking at our legs and started a game of 'Battleships and Cruisers' on our arms. Moles were battleships and freckles were cruisers, and there were points for guessing where they were under the dried mud. I always lost though, not because it was a law of nature, but because I had more moles and freckles than Reg.

'Reg. Why do you think someone like Poll might top herself?'

Reg looked uncomfortable. I think he knew where I was going.

'W-w-why does anyone? B-b-beats me.'

'If it was her, do you think it was because she didn't like what she did? Didn't like what she was?'

'Naah, Jimmy. Look around. There's h-h-hundreds, thousands of w-w-women workin' the p-p-pubs, d-d-drinkin' 'emselves s-s-senseless, and all the rest of it. And you know as well as I do that there's at least a d-d-dozen in our street. They're not all t-t-toppin' 'emselves, are they?'

'No, I suppose not.'

I could always rely on Reg for common sense.

I heard our front door rattle open and slam shut. A sailor straightened his collar and looked up and down the street before walking towards the pub. It was one of those rolling walks that sailors do after being at sea a long time. I knew this, but it still looked to me like a swagger.

The flag came down. Reg patted me on the back, mumbled, 'See ya, Jimmy,' and crossed over to his house.

I knew the moment I saw Mum. She hugged me and burst into tears.

'She wouldn't do that. Not Poll. Not in a million years. Not Poll.'

I felt hot tears drip on to my shoulder, and when there were none left I put away the half-empty gin bottle and made Mum a cup of tea. She sat at the kitchen table, shaking her head with her eyes closed.

'Not Poll,' she said over and again. 'Not Poll. She wouldn't kill herself. It's all a mistake. A big mistake. She must have had a terrible accident. Or been murdered.'

Chapter Eleven

I didn't sleep well that night. I kept falling into that half-asleep world where things that are real act like they're real until something unreal happens, which gets mixed up with the real and you don't know what's really real, if you follow me.

There was an explosion. I found myself alone in a stormy ocean at night. My ship and friends had gone. Black waves threw me and swallowed me and delivered me back to the surface, over and over and over. I flailed my arms and kicked my legs frantically but I had no control over anything. Just as I'd grabbed a half-breath I was pounded back, into the deep, over and over and over. Whipped by the wind, crushed by the waves.

I was losing.

Every crashing, crushing wave took my life away.

I was breathing water. Freezing water. It was filling my lungs. It was filling every cell of my body. Paralysing me. Until I felt nothing.

I wanted the mud. The warm mud. The safe mud.

I opened my eyes, relieved that it was over. The skull

was an inch away. Crabs started scuttling out of the cavernous eye sockets and spilling on to my face, their sharp legs and razor pincers pricking and jabbing and cutting my cheeks and lips and nose and forehead.

I screamed and pushed myself up out of the mud, trying to rip them off my face. As I screamed, one tore into my mouth and I pulled it out, retching and screaming. Then they dug at my eyes. I clawed at my face. And screamed.

I opened my eyes and moved my hands away from my face. Mum looked worried. She was gripping my shoulders.

'It's all right, Jimmy! Your ma's 'ere.'

I put my arms round her and held her tight. My nightshirt was cold and wet and clung to me like seaweed. My heart was pounding like a Dockyard steam hammer at full pelt.

'It's all right. It's over now. Your ma's here.'

I don't know how long we stayed like that because time at night plays tricks. But it seemed a long time and I felt safe. I hung on and smelt the Mum smell. No gin. Just Mum.

Then there were noises outside, getting louder. Somewhere, in the distance, crowds were cheering. Drunken people were singing and shouting. Glass was breaking.

'What's going on out there, Mum?'

She let go, got up off the bed and pulled back the curtain. The room lit up with the orange glow of the corner lamppost.

'I dunno, Jimmy. I couldn't sleep fer thinkin' about poor Poll. But there's a hell of a commotion out there that started up about an hour ago. P'rhaps the war's over, God willin'. There's 'undreds of people out on the streets. Queen's Street looks packed from 'ere. I daresay we'll know soon enough in the morning.'

She closed the curtain and kissed me on my wet forehead.

'Now, you try an' get some kip, Jimmy.'

'You too. Night, Mum.'

'Night-night, love.'

The next day I got up early. My nightshirt had dried on me, a reminder of my terrible nightmare. But I felt excited, and I didn't know why. Then I realized. The war. Was it really over? Or was that a dream? I got dressed quickly and ran over to Reg's.

Reg eventually opened the door with his eyes closed.

'W-w-what?'

'It's me.'

Reg isn't at his best in the morning. He opened his eyes.

'What's the time?'

''Bout seven o'clock.'

'Seven o'bleedin' clock? What the f-f-flippin' 'eck are you playin' at? G-g-go a'-bleedin'-way.'

I put my foot in to stop the door closing.

Reg groaned.

'Reg, didn't you hear all that noise last night? There

were crowds of people out in Queen's Street celebrating!'

I waited for the news to sink in.

'You m–m–mean we won the war?'

'Could be! Fancy runnin' down with me to the pier and gettin' the early edition? We could be the first in the street to know!'

Reg was dressed in two minutes.

'My eyes must be deceivin' me.' Jop rubbed his eyes and looked again, blinking his eyes in disbelief. 'The mudlark is, indeed, a rare sight in the early mornin'. What can account for this curious phenomenonononon? A terrible storm must 'ave upset its be'aviour patterns.'

'Very b–b–bleedin' funny, Jop.' It was still too early for Reg.

Jop smiled. 'Sorry, lads. I take it you want to read about last night?'

'Yes. Is it true? Is the war over?'

Jop picked up a copy and folded it.

'You'll 'ave to buy one to find out, Jimmy.' He winked. 'I got me livin' to make and times is 'ard. You'll understand the ebbs and flows of trade, bein' a fellow businessman. Things are pickin' up today, though!'

I laughed and handed over my penny.

Reg and I peered at the headlines and one thing was immediately obvious. The war was definitely not over. It was alive and well. The casualty list was longer than ever. And there were the usual heroes' stories and battle successes.

Jop sensed our disappointment. 'You're not the first

customers this mornin' to mistake the commotion last night with victory celebrations.'

'W-w-what w-w-was going on, then?'

Jop sighed. ''Fraid it's bad news. Not for me, but for them that's affected. Back page, under Stop Press.'

I turned the paper over and Jop pointed to it. The headline read 'Night Disturbances'.

'A number of disturbances were reported at the business establishments of alien residents last night . . .'

'W-w-what? Sorry, w-w-what's an alien resident?' Reg looked at Jop and then me.

Jop explained. 'They mean foreigners. Or I should say, people what 'as the misfortune of 'avin' foreign-soundin' names.'

'The police were powerless to prevent damage to the Albertolli Brothers' Swiss Café in Commercial Road, Hahn's Tailors of Queen's Street, Abraham's Jewellers of Palmerston Road, Greenbaum's bakery of Arundel Road, Horowitch's fishmongers of Ordnance Row and Vosbrugh's confectionary shop in Alfred Road . . .'

'No! Mr and Mrs Vosbrugh? Why would anyone want to do over their shop?'

I knew as soon as I said it. And I could tell from Reg's face that he knew. I remembered the look he'd given me in the Coliseum. The look he'd given me when I'd joined in the anger.

'Excuse me, lads.'

Jop signalled for us to move aside. There was a sudden rush and we stood back to let Jop's customers queue. The Dockyard shift was about to start and everybody wanted to read about the night's events. The pennies clinked into Jop's hand and the neatly folded papers were grabbed and instantly unfurled before their owners drifted down the pier towards the Dockyard Gate.

'We've got to go and see if there's anythin' we can do to help Mr and Mrs Vosbrugh.'

Reg nodded and patted me on the shoulder. He realized I felt guilty.

'Yeah, g-g-good idea, Jimmy.'

Chapter Twelve

Mr Vosbrugh was on his knees, crying. There's something about seeing a big man cry.

Mrs Vosbrugh had her hand on his shoulder and was staring at where the day's display of creamy toffees, slabs of fudge, bars of milky chocolate, chunks of cherry nougat and handmade chocolates should have been. And toffee apples. There should have been sticky, glistening toffee apples too.

The bay window was completely smashed in. Huge cobbles had been prised up from the road and thrown through it. The counter inside lay in a splintered heap. Sweet jars had been shattered against the wall and their contents trampled underfoot. Someone had tried to set fire to the interior and the walls were blackened. It hadn't caught, but the glorious, welcoming smell of sweet toffee had been replaced by the stench of hateful, acrid smoke.

As we got closer, Mr Vosbrugh's sobs got louder and I could feel broken glass under my bare feet.

The shop door lay flat on the pavement. A part of me wanted to get away from here, to open it and disappear.

On the brickwork beside the doorway, words were daubed in grey paint.

DeATH TO ThE HUn

It was the shade of grey they use in the Dockyard to paint battleships.

'We're sorry, Mrs Vosbrugh.'

Mrs Vosbrugh jumped nervously.

'Oh, lads. I am so sorry there are no toffee apples for you today. I am so sorry.'

'We . . . we wondered if we could help you.'

Mr Vosbrugh wiped his eyes on his shirt sleeve and stood up. He picked up the door, propped it up against the front of the shop and turned the sign to read 'CLOSED'.

Mrs Vosbrugh pointed to the grey-painted words. 'Why? I do not understand. We come from Belgium twenty years ago. We are like the British now. The Germans, they have invaded our country. That is why Britain is fighting them. I do not understand. I do not understand. I do not understand . . .'

Mr Vosbrugh put his arms round her.

'Why did people do this to us? I do not understand. I do not understand. The police . . . they watched. We plead with them, but they just watch. I do not understand. I do not understand.'

'We're so s-s-sorry, Mrs Vosbrugh. Is there anything we c-c-can do? We c-c-could help c-c-clear up. Have you got a c-c-couple of brooms?'

Reg had tears in his eyes.

Mrs Vosbrugh shook her head. 'No, lads. It is very kind of you. Very kind. But you would cut your feet with all this glass. It is everywhere. It is not a good idea.'

'But we want to help,' I pleaded. 'Our soles are thicker than clogs. We want to help. We really do.'

'No,' said Mrs Vosbrugh firmly. 'I do not want you to. This is something Hercule and I have to do. You are good lads. But we . . . we are very upset. Please, please, go home.'

She waved us away, and Reg and I left them surrounded by the wreckage. I felt so miserable. They wouldn't let us help, and I sensed that it was because, underneath, they thought we were like the mob that had ruined their business, the business they had spent twenty years building. What made it worse was that I had been part of the mob. Not that mob, but *a* mob. In the Coliseum. I had joined in. For a laugh.

Reg and I walked away. We didn't say anything to each other for ages. I guess it was the shock and, for me, the shame. We decided to go round to Archie's. We wanted to talk about it.

We turned into Barrack Street and saw Archie hopping about on the paving stones. It didn't look right, somehow. Undignified. Lillie was on the doorstep. Archie was obviously looking after her again and had renewed his attempt at teaching her hopscotch.

'So you throw the stone like this and then you hop and jump with both feet like this.'

But Lillie had learnt a new word.

'Why?'

'Because that's what you do. And then you twist round like this, and then hop and jump with both feet, on the numbers. Like this.'

'Why?'

Archie tried not to sound impatient. 'Because that's how you get back to where you started from, of course.'

We came up behind Archie, and Reg took up the questioning. There's nothing like a good wind-up.

'But w-w-why, Archie?'

Archie turned and looked embarrassed.

'Oh, it's you. How's things?'

'Don't ask. And stop trying to avoid the question. Lillie wants to know what the point of hopscotch is.'

I winked at Lillie.

'So do Lillie,' said Lillie, holding up rag-doll–Lillie.

There was a long silence while Archie thought.

'Well, what's the point of any game or sport?' he smiled triumphantly. 'I mean, what's the point of Pompey?'

Reg and I looked at each other. He'd got us.

'Good point. On current form, none at all.'

We all laughed and Lillie asked why.

At that moment the skies opened and we piled into Archie's front room and watched out the window as the chalk numbers slowly dissolved in the rain.

'You heard about last night, Archie?'

'Yeah. My ma said that some Germans got attacked. Spies and saboteurs. Serves 'em right, Hun scum!'

I reacted. 'That's just garbage, Archie. Mr and Mrs Vosbrugh spies? You must be jokin'. We just been round Alfred Street. It's terrible. The shop's totally wrecked. And so are Mr and Mrs Vosbrugh.'

Archie stood back, his chest inflated, his brow tight.

'Look. They were poisoning our bluejackets with chocolates. They deserve anythin' they get!'

'Absolute c–c–crap!'

Reg was getting angry. And so was I.

'Listen. They made special rum chocolates specially for our sailors. Straight up. Now ask yerself why.'

Archie stared at us to see the impact of his words. Reg and I smiled uneasily and shook our heads.

'They laced them with slow-acting poison and sold them to sailors joining the Grand Fleet. By the time they got there, they were sick or even dying. It's true. A bluejacket's aunty told my ma. Cunning, eh?'

I couldn't take any more.

'Bollocks, Archie! How can you say that? The Vosbrughs are Belgian. You know? The country we're defendin'!'

'Are you callin' my ma a liar?'

Lillie had been alerted by the angry voices and liked the sound of the new word.

'What's bollocks?'

Reg replied, staring at Archie. 'It's what your b–b–brother talks, Lillie.'

Archie's face twisted into something nasty. 'And you t–t–talk it every time y–y–you open y–y–your b–b–bloody g–g–gob–hole . . .' Archie pointed at him, sneering, and

Reg's fists clenched. ' . . . Y–y–you s–s–stuttering g–g–git!'

Archie had crossed the line.

'That's it, you b–b–bustard, outside!'

Reg stormed out into the pelting rain, closely followed by Archie. I stayed indoors and watched from the window. They squared up to each other on the pavement. The chalk numbers had disappeared. Water droplets flowed down the glass.

There was an exchange of insults, but I couldn't hear because of the hissing and drumming of the rain. Archie poked Reg in the chest and Reg headbutted Archie, who dropped like a sack of King Teds. He kicked Reg's legs away and Reg landed on his back with a sickening thud that I not only heard but felt. Pavement slabs are different from harbour mud.

Archie was on top of Reg, punching him in the stomach. Reg came back with a left hook, catching Archie on the chin. And so it went on. Blood came from noses and lips and it dripped on to the pavement and went brown and diluted and flowed into the gutter to join the chalk down the drain.

It should have been me out there, defending Mr and Mrs Vosbrugh. It should have been my blood.

Lillie climbed up on to the armchair beside me to see what was going on. She saw her brother punch Reg in the stomach and Reg give a classic uppercut back that took Archie off his feet again. She hugged rag-doll-Lillie as tightly as she could and then turned and asked, 'Why?'

Chapter Thirteen

The next morning Mum made me a special breakfast of fried egg and sausage. Grubb's sausages, Reg's favourite. I wondered how he was.

I'd taken him home and delivered him to his ma. He was in a terrible state. His ma took one look at him and screamed. Then she glared at me as if it was my fault.

The smell of a fried breakfast is the best start to a day. Mum took off her apron and I noticed she was dressed all in black. She told me she wasn't working today. She was going to Poll's funeral. Then she put her hand on the breakfast table as if she was steadying herself. Suddenly she looked older.

'Are you OK, Mum? Do you want me to come with you?'

In an instant she put on the bravest smile in the world.

'No, Jimmy. I'm OK. It's just . . . this is terrible . . . Poor Poll. They says that death comes in threes.'

Mum picked up her black hat and started pinning a black netted veil to the edge. What did that mean? Death comes in threes?

'That vicar wouldn't 'ave her in St Thomas's church-yard, cos of them sayin' it was suicide. Poor Poll . . . She's bein' buried at the Municipal Cemetery this mornin'.'

Mum was struggling with her anger.

'I'm sorry, Mum . . .'

'Yeah. Poll was a good lass. Full of fun. Full of life. We didn't want her put in no pauper's grave. Me and the sisters clubbed together and paid fer a proper, decent funeral. She's gonna be put to proper rest.'

'I'm so sorry, Mum.'

Mum had a lot of sisters, and they all looked after each other. If one was sick, the others would help her out. If they had troubles they shared them.

Poll hadn't jumped off the pier. Mum said she was full of fun, full of life, and that she would never do away with herself.

And who else had died? Mum said that death comes in threes.

Mum put on her black hat and adjusted it in the mirror. In the reflection I could see tears of anger and sorrow in her eyes. She pulled a bottle out of her hand-bag, took a long swig and stared at herself. Then she let down the black veil and hid her grief.

I needed to talk to her, but now was not the time.

Not yet.

I knocked at Reg's. It took an age for him to answer.

The door opened three inches.

'How are you, Reg?'

I could see a badly wrapped bandage around his head. He had two black eyes. Except they looked more blue than black. There was a long cut the length of his eyebrow, with three home-made stitches in the middle. His bottom lip was purple and swollen. His chin was grazed and there was a gap in his bottom teeth that hadn't been there before. The hand he held the door with was bruised and swollen.

'I'm f-f-fine, thanks, Jimmy.'

I nodded. 'Mudlarkin' today?'

'Er, n-n-no, I don't think so. I'll g-g-give it a miss today.'

'OK. See ya.'

'S-s-see ya.'

'Oh, Reg?'

'Yeah?'

I pulled a warm sausage out of my pocket and held it under his nose.

'Have a sausage. It's Grubb's. Made of the finest quality knackered old coppers.'

Reg smiled and started to laugh, but grimaced at the pain which turned the laugh into a groan.

'You bustard! Don't make me laugh! You did that deliberately.'

Reg took the sausage. I smiled and acknowledged my guilt.

'Yeah, OK. But it's only cos you're me mate. By the way, you did good.'

Reg smiled.

'Thanks.'

★

The pier was empty. Jop was adjusting his wooden leg. He looked in pain and was muttering to himself, 'Bleedin' arfritis.'

He spotted me and smiled.

'Hello, Jimmy! You on yer own? Where's yer mate today?'

'It's a long story. Reg and Archie had a bad ruck.'

Jop chuckled. 'Who won? I'd put my money on Archie. He looks an 'ard nut!'

'Nobody won. And they'll not be mudlarkin' for a while.'

Jop could tell it was serious and so he changed the subject.

'Well, watch out today, Jimmy. There's a bunch of mad posh ladies prowlin' round, handin' out white feathers. And they ain't fussy who they gives 'em to!'

He held up a white feather proudly and then nestled it back in between his medals.

'White feathers? Why?' I laughed.

'It's a tradition. A symbol of cowardice. They're tryin' to 'umiliate men into joinin' up. If you ain't in uniform, that's it, you gets one!'

'But that's flippin' daft!' I looked at Jop's wooden leg and medals.

He shook his head sadly and touched his temple with his forefinger. 'This war is sending people out of their attics, Jimmy.'

I thought about what had happened to Mr and Mrs Vosbrugh and I nodded.

'And this,' he held up a newspaper, 'is gettin' worse . . .'

Jop cleared his throat and shot a ball of phlegm over the platform. It dropped between the rails and hit the mud below with a distant slap.

He smiled his satisfaction and returned to the headlines, pointing them out one by one. They announced glorious victories in foreign towns and villages and ridges.

'If we're winning all these battles, here, there and everywhere, why do we 'ave so many bleedin' casualties?'

Jop wasn't expecting an answer – which was just as well because I didn't have one.

He turned to the list of casualties. It now covered a complete page. And the print was smaller so they could fit more in.

'I think you're starting to lack something in your sales technique, Jop.' I laughed, holding out my penny.

'I was merely pointin' out the in'erent contradictions. Of course it's worth every penny for the challenge and amusement it offers every reader in playin' Spot the Truth!'

He took my penny and delivered the folded paper into my palm.

'A bargain! Sold to the discerning young gentleman at the front!'

I sat alone in Fog Corner, turning the pages. The shift had just started and the men's smoke hung there, abandoned, with nowhere to go.

Jop was right. The newspaper was full of heroic deeds and wonderful victories written by so-called eyewitnesses who never seemed to see British soldiers being killed or defeated.

A headline caught my eye.

DOCKYARD WELCOMES ANOTHER ROYAL VISIT

King George, it said, had paid another one of his visits to the town and dropped in on the Dockyard to raise morale. I wondered how that worked. There you are, turning your spanner on a gun mount, when a king arrives, interrupts your vital war-work, and raises your morale. I turned the page, thinking that I must be missing something.

I studied the long list of those killed. Was my dad here today? I didn't think so. I was convinced that if he died I'd feel something at the moment he was killed. There must be some sort of link, something that connects us, even though he probably doesn't know I exist. I turned the page. A half-page appeal for recruits to the Portsmouth Chums Battalion. No chance. Then the sports page. Pompey had a Cup game with Woolwich Arsenal on Saturday. No chance. And there, beneath, in the Stop Press:

Nancy Wallace (29), of Britannia Road, a notorious woman of drunken habits, was found dead by police in her lodgings yesterday evening. The Police Superintendent reported that there were no suspicious circumstances and that a verdict of death due to natural causes was expected. The City Coroner duly concurred, saying that some people invited an early demise because of the way they chose to live.

I put the paper down on the bench. The smoke had cleared and a couple of little kids came in to pick out some dog-ends from the debris on the ground. They crawled under the bench and I could see that the soles of their feet were beginning to get thick and black like mine. They toughen up, the older you get. One screamed with glee when he found a packet of Woodbines that was half full. The other kid had some lucifers, so they sat down and lit up. They stared at me through narrowed eyes, concentrating hard on getting the smoking right.

I'd tried it myself a few times when I was their age, but couldn't see the point. Mum liked a smoke, but never outdoors, never in the street. That was dirt common. She was very careful about stuff like that. And not wearing red. And not having too much slap on.

The newspaper made me angry. Made me want to shout. Just because Nancy Wallace was a woman of so-called 'drunken habits' didn't mean she didn't count. And nobody really chooses to become like that, do they?

Not really.

I guess it just sort of happens.

I looked at the two kids.

They couldn't reach the ground from the bench, so they swung their legs like happy five-year-olds. But they had the dockie way with a cigarette. Corner of the mouth, dangling, or cupped in the hand to protect against the wind, even when you're indoors. Deep draws and a barely noticeable tap with a finger to release the ash.

When you're a kid you accept everything. Things are the way they are. Of course, Mum didn't choose. She had to work the pubs for the money, to keep our heads above water. She didn't have any other trade or skill. And she had to pay the rent without a man's wage. She had to do it so we could eat more than bread and dripping. And she had to do it so I could get a pair of boots one day.

She was doing it . . . It was all very clear to me now, clearer than it had been since I first realized what she did.

She was doing it . . . for me.

Chapter Fourteen

You don't get many coins tossed your way when you mudlark on your own; it doesn't take long to find that out. I persevered but only made three farthings in two and a half hours. I guess the punters like that element of competition. If you mudlark on your own, you're some sort of village idiot who's got stuck in the mud. People look straight ahead, the way kings and queens do on coins, determined not to catch your eye.

When you're on your own, you might get tossed the smallest small change out of sympathy, but would you want that? Well, I don't. I'm an entertainer. A performer. Not a beggar. No, never again, not on my own.

There was a smart civvie going down the pier. I noticed the pocket-watch chain and good-quality waistcoat and jacket. I decided to give it one last try. I decided to aim high.

'Throw us an 'alf crown, mister!'

He looked down at me, laughed, and said, very politely, without stopping, 'Get a job, sonny.'

Me and Reg were used to that sort of advice, though it

wasn't normally so polite. It usually came from pompous pen-pushers or paper-shifters. Reg reckoned it was envy. They didn't have a proper job themselves, and were envious of ours.

Today, I didn't answer back. I didn't know why, but it got to me a bit.

It got to me a lot.

But then I worked it out. Or admitted it.

I was thinking of Mum.

I had a job once. With Tippins the coal merchant in Unicorn Street. There were two problems. The first was that Mr Tippins thought he could tell me what to do. And the second was that coal wasn't nearly as much fun as mud. I went to lunch on my first day and was back mudlarking in the afternoon. I decided that that's what I was born to do. It was no use me fighting it. Nothing was going to change the fact that I was, am and always would be a mudlark.

Always?

That's a long time.

I stood at the water's edge and looked at my three farthings. I couldn't take them home to Mum. It was just too pathetic. Is this all I was worth?

What if I got a job? What if I earned a regular wage? Then Mum could pack in her pub work and her drinking. The two went together like salt and vinegar, bread and dripping, mud and mudlarks. If she could afford to give up her pub work, she wouldn't drink the way she does.

Some seagulls were staring at me from the barnacle-encrusted struts under the pier. Their calls in the wind sounded like laughter. Were they mocking me because I was only worth three miserable farthings?

I rinsed the coins, one by one, as the water licked my feet. The first I guessed was a Vic, but it was a Ted. The second I guessed was a Ted, but it was a Vic. I was sure the third was a Ted, but it was a George.

The laws of nature hadn't changed.

The royal heads were staring into the distance, like there was something really interesting on the horizon. They refused to look me in the eye, and then they laughed at me too. I heard them. Even Queen Vic joined in. She who was never amused.

But then again it was probably the seagulls.

I stooped and skimmed King George as hard as I could. I wanted to make him laugh on the other side of his pompous, stuck-up face. I hoped his medals weighed him down. He bounced seven times before disappearing under the waves. Goodbye, George.

My record for stones was six. I smiled at my discovery. Coins were much better than the flattest of stones. I took another run-up. King Ted managed nine. Ta-ta, Ted. I couldn't top that, surely? An extra long run-up, an extra flick of the wrist, and Victoria was unstoppable, going on and on, far out into the harbour for at least fifteen before I lost count of the little skips at the end. Bloody perfect. The laughter stopped. That'll teach her.

I jumped up with my arms stretched to the sky,

shouting across the harbour, 'Champion of the world!!!'

The seagulls took off in alarm.

This was a record, a new world record.

But then I realized that it didn't count. There wasn't anyone to share it with.

At least I didn't think so, until I heard a heavy clapping from the pier. I looked up. Jop was leaning on the railings and smiling broadly.

'Well done, Jimmy lad! I thought that one was goin' on a one-way trip to Gosport!'

'Hello, Jop! You saw it! Yeah, it was pretty damn good, wasn't it?!' I tried not too hard to sound modest. 'How many did you count?'

'Well, from up 'ere I saw seventeen, but there was probably more!'

'I'll be up in a minute to sign autographs if you can keep the excited crowds in order.'

I began to climb the struts up to the pier. Jop leant over and watched me.

'Tell you what, Jimmy, next Olympics, you and me!'

'Me and you?'

Jop winked. 'You skimmin' and me gobbin' fer Great Britain. Two golds in the bag. The rest of the world acknowledges the superiority of the British and throws their 'ands up in surrender. A grateful nation salutes us and we gets personally thanked and knighted by King George 'imself.'

Jop reached out and helped pull me up over the railing. I was pleased I could share my record with him. And he could verify it with my mates. That would be the next best thing to a knighthood.

There was no pile of the midday newspaper beside Jop, and his cash bag was bulging larger than I'd ever seen it. And he had written 'Sold Out' on a piece of old cardboard and hung it on the railings.

'No need to ask how business is today then, Jop?'

'No, Jimmy, not today. Mind you, I'd rather have not sold a single copy, what with the terrible news.'

My world record was forgotten.

'What terrible news? What's happened?'

Jop turned and looked out of the harbour at Spithead. In the distance, white triangles, silent and tranquil, were sailing against the grey backdrop of the Isle of Wight.

'The *Good Hope*. She's gone down.'

'Christ.'

'Blown up by the *Scharnhorst*.'

I started thinking about my mates whose dads and older brothers were serving on the *Good Hope*. She was a Portsmouth ship and most of the crew were from Portsea. Last August half the town had turned out to wave them off with white handkerchiefs and Union Jacks. Wives and mothers and sisters and grandmothers and brothers and sons and fathers. The bluejackets had lined the deck in their straw hats, standing to attention, while a band on the Hard played 'Onward Christian Soldiers'. Except that we all sang 'Onward Christian Sailors, sailing off to war . . .'

'How bad?'

'Bad.'

'How many?'

'Nine hundred.'

'Jesus Christ.'

'The telegram boys are going to be busy today.'

It was a long time before either of us said anything more. Jop carried on collecting his stuff up. Nine hundred. That was probably everybody on board.

Jop was ready to go.

'The Admiralty 'ave been sittin' on the news for days, but they 'ad to come clean in the end. They couldn't cover that one up.'

Jop adjusted his notice, tied his cash bag to his belt, and we walked slowly to the pierhead. Every time Jop's wooden leg clunked on the pier deck, the seagulls that lined the railings closest to us broke ranks and flew off into the harbour, crying. I kept remembering the face of a kid at school or a neighbour or a friend who had heard the news today. I tried to imagine what they were going through.

Was I lucky? Was it better never to have known your dad? Or was it better to have known and loved your dad, only for him to get killed?

Halfway up the pier and Jop broke the rhythm to catch his breath. He was wheezing quite badly.

'You know, they reckon every seagull is a lost sailor's soul.'

I believed it. The way they neatly lined the pier railings like the bluejackets on the deck of the *Good Hope*.

'That's why they keep crappin' on me cos they know I'm an old soldier.'

He tapped his medals and smiled.

I smiled too.

'Us soldiers, you know, our souls become rats. That's what I'll be soon.'

It sounded like he was looking forward to it. I can think of worse things. Coming back as a slug, or a head-louse or a copper. No, I'd happily settle for being a rat.

Jop looked out as the last of the seagulls launched themselves up and out, circling the harbour, soaring high and swooping low. We thought about all those sailors.

Jop watched with eyes that were starting to fill with water. He dabbed them with his cuff in one movement, embarrassed, as if he was mopping his brow.

'They're free now,' he said.

'Free as the wind!'

Chapter Fifteen

The shops in Queen's Street were almost deserted. The greengrocer's trays propped up on the pavement were full of winter vegetables, coated in heavy clay soil. Mum never bought her veg from Mr Lodge. She said that they cost the earth when Mr Lodge weighed them, and that he was a trickster. And that she had enough mud coming in the house already, thank you very much.

But nobody was buying today.

It was the same at Vosper's bakery. Dozens of unsold loaves were stacked up in the window. The bakery chimney was smokeless, the ovens had been turned off and there wasn't the usual glorious smell of freshly baked pastries and ginger biscuits.

Some shops had shut and had the blinds pulled down out of respect. Grubb's the butchers had a hand-written one up with bloody brown fingerprints all over it. It said: 'Business as Usual'.

In the distance I could hear the Dockyard at work. The tragedy had not stopped the whoosh and thud of the steam hammers, the hum of electricity generators, the clanging of metal and the deep singing of men as they hammered the rivets home. Ships were the dockies' babies, and they wanted revenge for the *Good Hope*. It wasn't just 'Business as Usual'. It was personal now. Every rivet was a bullet aimed at Kaiser Wilhelm's heart.

An empty tram slowly rattled by, heading for the Hard. On the top deck the conductor was reading the war headlines. The paper kept tugging away from one hand and sticking to his face, and he kept pushing it away to arms' length. On the bottom deck there was just one passenger. He had his collar turned up and a cloth cap pulled forward, but there was something familiar about his profile, framed by the window of the tram. It took a few seconds for it to come to me. Was that King George? King George, on a tram in Portsea? No, it was just too stupid. I knew he'd visited the town, but he wouldn't get about on a Corporation tram! I blinked to refocus, but the tram and its passenger had gone.

From the east, I heard a policeman's whistle, clear and shrill. And I counted. They were all short blasts, which meant it was serious. Petty crimes were coded in long ones.

One short blast meant a murder . . . two meant a riot . . . three short, that meant a burglary, four, a serious accident or fire . . . It stopped at five. Five. The same number as when we found the skull. Poll's skull.

Two policeman trotted past me and turned into Albert Street. They were both old and unfit. The slower one left a trail of puffs of smoke from a pipe that was clenched between his teeth as he ran, reminding me of a clapped-out old steamer on its way to the breaker's yard, up-harbour.

By quickening my pace I could easily keep up with them. What did five short whistles mean? I had to be careful. With so few people about I could easily be spotted.

They turned east into Curzon Row and I followed, cautiously, about twenty yards behind. The curtains were drawn in the front windows of some of the terraced houses I passed. It's the Portsea tradition when there's a death in the family. Behind those curtains they were keeping the world out. The world had killed their sons or husbands, and it could go to hell. At least I guessed that's what they thought. That's how I'd feel.

The whistle blasts became louder. We were getting close. Probably in the next street.

'Oy, you!'

The shout came from behind me. I turned. Another copper was heading straight for me. He'd seen me following the others. His thick truncheon was gripped in his right hand. I could feel the pavement slabs juddering under my feet. He was coming at me fast, raising his truncheon high. I could see the grain in the polished wood against the sky. Instinct and reflex took over. I stepped aside and jumped to where he had just been. He twisted and fell, caught between where he wanted to go and where his weight was taking him. Ha!

Once I'm at full sprint there's no stopping me. No man on earth – and certainly no Portsea copper – can touch me. My toes hit the pavement like it's not there. I fly faster than the wind off the Solent. My legs pump stronger than a locomotive at full steam. My fists piston the air like it's not there. My brain feels but doesn't think. I feel more alive than life. I feel like I'm not there. I'm gone.

I found myself in Queen's Street. My body was catching up with what I had done. While I leant over with my hands on my knees, catching my breath, I thought about what had happened.

Five short blasts.

I spat into the gutter and straightened up.

It could mean there had been a suicide, but I didn't believe it.

I wanted to get back home, to see Mum. I would talk to her today. Definitely. I would tell her how much her working the pubs and her drinking worried me. And I would tell her that I was going to try to get a job with a regular wage, so that she wouldn't have to do what she did.

Reg would understand. He wouldn't like it, but he would understand. Anyway, I could still mudlark in my spare time. I would still be a mudlark.

I turned out of Queen's Street into Keppel's Road. There were five houses with drawn curtains in Keppel's Road, three in Britannia Street, seven in Albion Row, nine in Victoria Terrace. I wanted to cross over to the other side of the road every time I saw one. I could feel the grief leaking out through those houses and I walked faster so that I wouldn't catch it.

Suddenly there was a scream of rubber on granite. Sam the Telegram braked his bike hard in the gutter beside me. He nearly came over the handlebars, and bundles of yellow envelopes fell into the gutter and split open on impact, spreading them all over the road. Sam swore and propped his bike up against the kerb.

'Hello, Sam! How's things?' Stupid question.

'Busy ain't the word, as you can see!' We looked at the scattered telegrams and began gathering them up and tying them back together with hairy string.

'I gets a penny bonus for every one I delivers. Great, ain't it!'

He was actually smiling.

'Jesus, I couldn't do your job, Sam.'

'Oh, you gets used to it,' Sam explained breezily. 'All you does is knock the door and give the envelope to whoever answers. Sometimes it's more than one envelope. Two birds wiv one stone. Once I 'ad four for one address. Fourpence for knockin' a door! Then you rides off. That's it. Money fer old rope!'

I knew that sons sometimes joined the same ships as their dads, but four in one family? A father and three sons? It was just too terrible.

'Well, I couldn't do it. Facing all them widows and orphans.'

Sam shrugged as he stuffed some of the bundles back into the sack.

'I reckon I'm gonna make nearly four quid today.'

'Blood money,' I said in my head. But it came out loud, and Sam reacted. He angrily snatched the bundle I was holding.

'Well, p'rhaps you can afford to be all hoity-toity with yer begged mud money and the dosh your ma fleeces from the sailors. Well, I ruddy well can't, see?'

I wanted to hit him for mentioning Mum, but I let it go. We were quits.

'Since Mr Vosbrugh's shop got wrecked and him and his missus got arrested, I ain't earned nothing from . . .' He looked up and down the street. 'You know, from the saucy pics.'

I didn't know the Vosbrughs had been arrested. As if what had happened to them wasn't bad enough. I could feel my teeth clenching at the injustice.

'Yeah, they're lockin up 'undreds of aliens in the prison and police cells. They're getting' an old liner ready fer 'em. It's gonna be moored up 'arbour. Internment they calls it. Just like they did with convicts when we was at war with that Frenchy Boney Part geyser an 'undred years ago.'

'People still don't really think they're spies, do they? That's barmy!'

Jop was right. The war was sending people mad.

'I know, but what can you do? Mr Vosbrugh's an 'armless old bloke and he was good to me. And to the soldiers and sailors. He's very patriotic, you know.'

I didn't suppose Mr Vosbrugh thought Britain was quite so great now. I'm damn sure I wouldn't.

Sam pushed the sack upright into the saddlebag and prepared to kick off.

'Can't stop. Time's money. See you around!'

'Yeah, see ya.'

Sam wobbled off to ruin more lives. I'm being hard on him, Sam's all right really. He just hasn't got much feeling or imagination in him. Perhaps he's lucky. If I was him, I'd pedal off over Portsdown Hill and never come back. Perhaps I'm gutless. But then someone has to deliver the death telegrams. If it was down to me, they'd never get them, and that would be worse.

But not knowing?

Is that worse?

Like me not knowing about my dad?

There's something reassuring about your own street. No matter what's happening in the world, in the war or in Portsea, it's your street, your territory. You know where you are. Everything is familiar and in its place and a part of you.

The flag was down. It was time to speak to Mum.

I went round the back alley.

Mum wasn't there doing the chores. She wasn't there to laugh and point the finger and accuse me of mud-larking. The tin bath stayed on the hook in the backyard.

I turned the back-door latch.

Where was the smell of hot dinner? Or the hot steam of laundry? There was usually one or the other, some-times both; but today, nothing. There wasn't even that unmistakable smell of your home that you don't get in anyone else's, and I was beginning to wonder whether I could trust my senses.

The house was silent. Where was Mum?

'Mum?'

I looked through to the kitchen and saw her slumped over the table.

'Mum?'

Chapter Sixteen

Mum was resting her head on her arms on the kitchen table. I thought she was asleep but then I noticed her shoulders were gently moving up and down. There was a dead gin bottle lying on its side and another one, half alive, beside it.

'Mum?'

She turned and opened her mouth, but no words came. Her face was red. Tears streamed down her cheeks and dripped on to the newspaper that was spread out over the table. I had never seen Mum cry before. Not like this.

I bent down and put my arms round her, and she clutched me, sobbing.

'Oh, Jimmy. I'm so sorry.'

'Sorry, Mum? Why?'

'All 'ands lost. All 'ands lost. All 'ands . . .'

She howled and buried her face in my chest and I hugged her tightly. I didn't know what to say. She kept saying she was sorry, so sorry, so very sorry, and clung on to me; and I hung on to her, saying that it was all right, that everything would be all right.

The newspaper on the table was blotched with tears and circles of gin. I read the headline.

Encounter with *Scharnhorst*.
Good Hope lost.
No survivors.

Mum let go and dabbed her eyes with a handkerchief.

'I've got to talk to you, Jimmy. I've been meanin' to talk to you fer a long time. But now ... now it's too late ...'

Her lips trembled, but she steeled herself and looked directly into my eyes.

'I've been meanin' to tell you about yer dad, Jimmy.'

'My dad? But I 'aven't got a dad.' There was a long silence. I realized she was about to confess something.

I didn't think Mum knew who he was. I thought he was one of her long-gone and forgotten soldier or sailor friends, like Reg's. And I never, ever asked. I didn't want to upset her by asking. I just assumed, you know?

I sat down at the kitchen table. I was supposed to be talking to Mum. Trying to persuade her to give up the drinking and the pub work. And telling her that I was going to try to get a job, a real job with a regular wage.

And now she was talking to me about my dad.

My dad.

Mum was calm now.

'I have to tell you, Jimmy. I have to ... explain. I was a young lass, not much older than you, and I worked as a scullery maid in a big 'ouse in Southsea. This was in the naughty nineties.'

It was good to see her smile after being so upset.

'But I tell you there wasn't any naughtiness in my creek of the 'arbour. Then, just after the start of the new century, Queen Vic popped her clogs at Osborne 'ouse, over the Island. People was cryin' in the streets. Couldn't understand why. She always struck me as a sour-faced old cow.'

Mum smiled again, and I smiled too.

'The fleet gathered at Spithead to show their respects. Everyone turned out to watch 'em firin' their gun salute as 'er body was carried across the Solent in the Royal Yacht. That was a bleedin' racket. After 'er coffin was put on a train to London, all the bluejackets from them ships come ashore. And, fer me sins, I fell in love wiv one of 'em.'

This was a surprise. No, a shock. I didn't know what to think, what to feel.

'You mean, you really . . . really, like . . . loved him?'

Mum was surprised at my surprise.

'Of course I did. His name was James. I named you after 'im. You're my little bit of 'im.'

Mum's face lit up at the memories, and I could see the girl who fell in love.

'He 'ad lovely blue eyes. As blue as the Solent on a summer day.'

She looked into my eyes.

'You've got his eyes, Jimmy. I only 'ad to look into 'em an' I was drownin'.'

I wanted to hear more about him. I wanted to know what he was like.

'And when he was out of uniform he was very smart. Yeah, James was a nifty dresser . . .'

'Bit like me then,' I laughed.

Mum looked at my muddy clothes and laughed too.

'No, but you've got 'is sense of 'umour, Jimmy.'

She told me everything. How he was already married to someone, out Fratton way. How he broke Mum's heart. How she went to pieces, lost her job at the big house because she was pregnant with me, couldn't get another job in service and ended up on the streets.

She picked up the half-alive bottle and toasted, 'Medicine for a broken 'eart!' and took several long, deep gulps.

'Did he, did my dad, did he know . . . about me?'

I had to know. It was important. I took away the bottle and put it on the floor.

Mum looked down at the newspaper, blotted with tears.

'I'm sorry, Jimmy. No. And he won't never do now.'

A surge of anger shot from my heart to my mouth. I was beginning to understand. I was beginning to realize.

'Why didn't you tell him? Were you ashamed of me?'

'NO! I just couldn't. He'd gone by the time I knew that I 'ad you inside me.'

Another surge. Her stink of gin hit my nostrils. Suddenly it disgusted me.

'He died on the *Good Hope*, didn't he, Mum?' I shouted. It was an accusation.

Mum nodded and pointed to one name in the sea of small print.

'I'm sorry, Jimmy.'

I let the admission reach my brain and realized something.

I had been betrayed.

'That's it then, is it? After fourteen years of not knowing, you tell me who my dad is.

'You tell me how wonderful he is. And then you tell me he's dead!'

'I'm sorry, Jimmy. I couldn't tell him, and I couldn't tell you. I can understand you bein' angry, but you 'as to understand . . .'

'Well, I don't bloody well understand. How could you do that?' I could feel the confusion in my head, forcing out years of anger, years of tears. I fought it, but my face burst and I screamed, 'How could you do that?! I could have known him! How could you do that?!'

Mum opened her mouth but she couldn't say anything. She couldn't look at me. She dropped her head and covered her face with her hands and she sobbed.

I slammed the back door behind me, punched the tin bath off the wall and kicked the yard gate shut. I could have known him. I could have known my dad.

My dad.

I walked hard, hands clenched, striding fast. Didn't matter where. I was OK if I walked hard, if I didn't stop.

I had to get away; but I could hear footsteps behind me, following me, haunting me, but when I turned there was no one there.

I went where the pavements took me, not looking up, crossed roads, not looking up, turned corners, not looking up. The pavements were wet. I didn't know where I was going, it didn't matter where. All that mattered was that I could have known him. Known my dad.

My dad.

I just needed to walk and not look up. I'd be all right if I didn't stop. I'd be all right if I could know him. I walked and walked and walked. Those footsteps were still behind me, keeping up, but I thought they must be in my mind. My dad's ghost?

The shadows got longer and the wet pavements flickered orange as lampposts came on. Water dripped from my face. She should have told me. I should have known him. Known my dad.

My dad.

Who's dead.

I didn't know where I was going, where I was or where I'd been. It didn't matter. My feet and my mind ached and I couldn't feel anything in between. More and more people were around, but I didn't look up. They got out of the way like sail to steam. Perhaps they knew. It was just as well cos I swear I'd have clocked anybody who said anything to me, anybody who got in my way, anybody, anybody who had a dad. Clock 'em hard because I hadn't, didn't and never would have one.

I heard the whine and clatter of trams and sensed the

warmth of more and more people and pubs and cafés. Light from their windows crossed the wet pavements before me. The same patterns, over and over. I was going around and around.

Then I stopped and bent down, putting my hands on my knees. I was cried out.

I closed my eyes, brought my head up and opened them again. It looked like the Town Square. But was I somewhere else? I didn't know where, but somewhere far away, where you can't get betrayed or hurt?

I was standing on the steps of the Town Hall. I looked up. Between two marble pillars a canvas banner hung like a twisted hammock, with the twisted words 'Join the Portsmouth Chums Battalion'. A sodden Union Jack clung to its pole on the roof. Above, the clock in the tower was coming up to eleven. I sat down on the steps and leant against the plinth under one of the stone lions. I closed my eyes and the bustle of the square gradually subsided to become the familiar sound of the sea on a calm day.

There was an explosion that shook the ship away, and I found myself in an ocean that was suddenly, violently stormy. I had been here before, except this time I wasn't alone. There was a man struggling with me, beside me. I couldn't see his face. It was night, and black waves threw us and swallowed us and delivered us back to the surface of the water, over and over and over. I reached out to hold him, but he kept slipping away. I touched his fingertips. An iron hand gripped my shoulder and held me back. I hit out, flailing my arms and kicking my legs frantically. I had to save him. But they were stopping me.

Chapter Seventeen

I knew that smell. Disinfectant and piss. I opened my eyes but didn't recognize the ceiling. It was rocking to and fro, so I curled up into a ball and waited for the explosion and the storm.

But nothing happened. And the back of my head hurt like hell. I put my hand on it and felt the swell and wetness of a wound. The blood had congealed in my hair, making it a sticky clump. This wasn't a dream.

I sat up and immediately felt dizzy for a few seconds. Then the rocking subsided. I realized where I was. The brown-tiled walls were glossy and I could see my black silhouette reflected and distorted in them. I refocused and saw that the tiles were covered with scratched and engraved words. Dates, names, hate words and love hearts. One word, bigger than the rest, was 'Mum'.

The cell was small and cold. I could see my breath filling it and condensing on the tiles. There was no window or bars, just a small hatch in a solid, riveted metal door. From behind it, somewhere, there was movement, and men's cries and then, further away, echoes of men's cries. On the floor beside me was a piss pot, full to the brim, with a dead spider floating on the surface. Its thick legs were splayed out, like it was reaching out for help or fighting back or surrendering. I shuddered.

I went over what had happened. What did I remember? I'd walked for, I guess, about six hours and I reckon I fell asleep on the Town Hall steps. I figured that the coppers must have picked me up, thinking I was a tramp. They don't like tramps much.

Ruddy cheek. It's almost as bad as being called a beggar. I'd get fined ten bob by the magistrate in the morning. Mum'd be angry, but I didn't care. It might help her to see that what she did was wrong. But I was still angry. And I wanted her to see that she was wrong.

I walked over the cold stone floor to the door and felt the soreness of my feet. The cold numbed the pain a bit, but they still hurt. The metal hatch was closed, but there was a narrow gap between its hinges. I stood on the tips of my toes, stretching the blisters on my feet and making the pain worse. Outside, in a narrow corridor, there were dozens of miserable-looking men shuffling by in single file. They were so close that if the door hadn't been there and their heads weren't bowed, I'd have felt their breath. They were prisoners, like me.

Except they weren't like me. They were being taken somewhere else. Suddenly my heart leapt and then sank. A familiar face! Or was it? It looked like Mr Vosbrugh, but with his head down it was difficult to tell. And he looked so much smaller. I opened my mouth to say something, but I couldn't. I wanted to shout that I was on his side. That I was sorry about what was happening. But by the time I was sure it was him and I'd worked out what to say, he'd gone. To be locked up, I supposed, on a ship in the harbour, like Sam had said.

Then the last prisoner passed by, and as he did so I realized it was Mr Berlusconi the pawnbroker. I felt sorry for him too, despite his attitude over the boots. The corridor went quiet. Every few minutes, policemen would walk by, the nails in their boots cracking on the stone slab floor, sometimes alone, sometimes in pairs. I caught words of conversation, and I listened, hoping I would find out what was going to happen to me. One had a son fighting in Belgium and his missus was knitting some socks to send him. Another hoped he didn't have cheese in his lunch-box today. Another sneezed, and the noise echoed down the corridor like an explosion. And another said that the woman who had been murdered yesterday was the seventh so far. I put my ear to the hatch, but the creaking and clanging of a door prevented me hearing any more, except for a name that was whispered, quietly but clearly, at the end of the corridor. The name was Jack the Ripper.

I sat back down on the bunk.

Seven murders? Jack the Ripper?

Jesus.

But Jack the Ripper did his murders twenty-five years ago, in London, eighty miles away.

I had to get back home. There was a madman out

there. I needed to warn Mum. Anything could happen to her while I was locked up.

'Let me out!' I shouted down the corridor. 'Please, I must see my mum!'

I hammered on the steel door, but it was so thick and solid that my fists didn't make a sound.

'Please, let me out!'

Nobody came. Nobody let me out.

But then I heard a familiar voice.

'J-J-Jimmy?'

It was Reg! He was in one of the cells at the other end of the corridor. I tried to see out of the gap.

'Reg! They got you too, then. Are you all right?'

'Yeah. I suppose.'

He sounded miserable, and I knew why. It was my fault, all my fault.

'I'm sorry, Reg. I'm sorry about the boots. But we've got to get out of here! We've got to warn my mum and the other sisters. Did you hear? Jack the Ripper's out there! He's back!'

Before Reg could reply, there was the sound of approaching footsteps and the heavy rattle of keys. Two policemen marched by and hauled Reg out of his cell. I saw his face for a second as he was marched back.

'Reg! Warn Mum!'

But he was gone. I banged on the door again with my fists as hard as I could, but it was futile. My knuckles were raw and bleeding but I couldn't feel any pain. I slumped down on the bunk and closed my eyes.

The police whistle code of five short blasts must be used for the Jack the Ripper murders. But it didn't make sense. Why were they being reported as suicides? Why was it being hushed up?

The cells were silent and I lost all sense of time and where I was. I was woken by more footsteps, this time fast and heavy, and the metal door shook, a key was turned and the bolt shot back. The door opened, and two stocky policemen stood in the doorway. One had a bushy moustache and a truncheon which he rhythmically tapped into his cupped palm.

'Now then, lad, you behave yerself and you won't get any more of this.'

I felt the back of my head. There was no need for it. No need for any of this.

The other policeman rattled his keys as he slipped the thick iron keyring over his knuckles and gripped it in his fist like a knuckleduster. He saw my fear and smiled.

I stared back at them. It occurred to me that they would be better employed fighting Germans somewhere. With them on your side, it'd be over by Christmas. And I don't think they'd take any prisoners.

They grabbed my arms, one each side, and marched me out the door and through a labyrinth of brown-tiled corridors to a spot in front of the sergeant's desk. I recognized this part of the station. I looked up, and King George was still on the wall with his medals. The sergeant picked up his pen and cleared his throat without looking at me.

'Name?'

For a second I thought about saying Archie's name. Reg would appreciate that. I worked out the odds of getting away with it. If it was a caution, there might be a good chance, but this was going all the way. So it didn't really matter.

'Charlie Chaplin.'

The sergeant looked at me for the first time.

'James Hunter. I want you to tell me your name.'

So he remembered me from before. And he knew my name.

'If you think you know my name, why are you asking?'

'There are procedures. What's your name?'

I stared at him and kept my mouth tightly shut.

'You didn't think you'd get away with it, did you?'

He didn't expect an answer.

'James Hunter, you are charged with the theft of seven pairs of police boots.'

He turned to the policeman with the tapping truncheon.

'I believe we have additional charges for this prisoner?'

The policeman slotted his truncheon into a long pocket on the inside of his uniform jacket and pulled a notebook out of his breast pocket.

'The prisoner was followed from Jubilee Terrace, after which he behaved in a very suspicious manner. After going around in the streets of Portsea several times the prisoner curled up on the Town Hall steps with the obvious intention of spending the night there. Vagrancy.'

I shook my head.

'Nah. That won't stick. I was just restin' my eyes.'

I smiled. Jop would appreciate that one.

I didn't see the cuff coming, but I felt it soon enough. It caught me on the back of my head, right on the gash, and I cried out. Then I felt blood trickling down the back of my neck.

The sergeant repeated the charge slowly as he wrote it down.

'Why are you wastin' your time pickin' on me when Jack the Ripper's in Portsea, killin' women? All you're worried about are a few old boots!'

The sergeant glared at me but didn't reply. He turned to the policeman with the notebook.

'Anything else? I do hope there's something else.'

The policeman glanced at his notebook.

'Upon his arrest, the prisoner swore at me. Abusive language.'

My head hurt but I couldn't resist it. 'That's bloody ridiculous.'

I felt the air move and I flinched, but it still hurt. Worse this time, but I stopped myself from crying out, just to show them.

The sergeant dipped his pen in an inkwell and wrote down the second charge.

'Some people never learn. Anything else?'

The policeman turned a page in his notebook and shrugged. 'He tried to push me away when we woke him up, so I suppose, resisting arrest.'

'I never! That's rubbish. These bustards hit me awake, then hit me unconscious!'

I put my hand up to my head just in time and deflected the cuff, but the policeman with the keys kicked away my legs and I fell to the stone floor.

'Bustard!'

The sergeant looked down at me.

'Resisting arrest? I think we can stretch that to assaulting a police officer in the course of his duty. And the prisoner also appears to be unsteady on his feet. Drunk and disorderly.'

The pen dipped and scratched and scratched.

The policeman with the notebook snapped it shut and the one with the keys hauled me up with a meaty hand. The sergeant removed his spectacles.

'Thank you. You've made our job very easy. You can't say you weren't warned, but I'm afraid your curiosity has caught up with you. You and your accomplice are thieves, but, more importantly, you are a menace, pokin' your nose in where it's not wanted. And we're going to throw the book at you. It's a big, heavy book and you'll know when it hits you.'

He looked at me for a response. I didn't give him one but stared back impassively. Me, a menace? What did he mean?

'I wouldn't like to be in your shoes, James Hunter.'

I could feel tears building up, but I wasn't going to show them. They were stitching me up tighter than a kipper's corset and then throwing away the needle. But I wasn't going quietly.

'I don't have any shoes, you bustard!'

I spat the last word out and it stopped the tears coming.

The smack hit the same place and made me feel dazed, like I was somewhere else. The last thing I remembered was the sergeant looking down at my feet and smiling.

'It's only a matter of time, lad. Only a matter of time.'

Chapter Eighteen

The magistrate was so old he looked like a tortoise. The bench he sat at was brown and polished like a coffin. The wooden box I was standing in felt like one too. It had iron spikes around it, probably to stop anyone climbing out.

My head was hurting like hell and I felt strange, like I didn't exist.

It took a little while to realize that Reg was standing next to me. I smiled and nodded to him just in case it wasn't a dream. His face was covered in cuts and bruises and I reckoned the police had beaten him up too, but then I remembered his scrap with Archie. He nodded back but didn't smile. He looked worried.

The tortoise yawned his way through the trial. His mouth kept turning from a crooked, no-lipped crack into an ugly, toothless hole. I knew that no good would come out of it.

Mr Berlusconi, the pawnbroker, suddenly appeared in the witness box and seemed to be answering some questions. He looked worried but very eager to help. The next time I looked, Archie was standing there. I smiled at him and waved, but he looked away guiltily. It was a big surprise to see Archie there, but things like that happen in my dreams. His mouth was moving, so I listened.

'No, they're not my friends, as such. I just 'appen to sort of know them, sir. I would not associate with thieves, sir.'

Then I was aware of Reg shouting at him and the magistrate pointing at Reg and telling him to be quiet or he'd regret it.

I listened to the policemen in their crisp white shirts swearing on the Bible to tell the truth, the whole truth and nothing but the truth. Then they lied through their yellow graveyard teeth.

I kept reassuring myself that I wasn't here, that this wasn't happening, that the dizziness and ache in my head somehow meant I was somewhere else. I wasn't in a coffin, but in my bed. My ship had gone down and I was drowning in a dream. I'd wake up soon and everything would be all right.

'I find the defendants um . . .'

The tortoise stretched out his neck and his dull black pin eyes slowly moved across the papers laid out in front of him. He was looking for something, then found it.

'Um . . . Reginald Ronson and James Hunter . . . guilty of all charges.'

The word 'guilty' brought him alive. I saw his flicker-ing, thin, pink tongue for the first time and noticed his pin eyes gleaming. I gripped two of the spikes that lined the dock and felt their coldness. I squeezed them hard until it hurt, and I knew that the court was real and that Reg and I were in real trouble. Reg had his head in his hands.

I had to do the right thing. It was all my fault. I was the guilty one.

'I talked Reg into thievin' the boots!'

Nobody took any notice.

'It was all my fault! He didn't want to do it!'

The magistrate shuffled his papers and cleared his throat.

'I would like to take this opportunity to commend the police for their handling of this case. We live in difficult times. The Hun is proving a dastardly enemy, and there's nothing our brave, brave soldiers and sailors would find more comforting than to know that law and order is being preserved at home. It is these civilized values that they are gallantly fighting for on land and sea . . .'

He knew this speech off by heart, and I wondered how many times he'd delivered it. He was relishing every word and was eager to get to the sentencing.

'The prisoners are guilty of the theft of property, and of assaulting the defenders of these civilized values. Police intelligence reports that they are beggars and represent a public nuisance of the worst kind. Neither have ever been gainfully employed. What a waste of youthful energy! It is established that they belong to that sad breed of fatherless children that has never known a decent upbringing or proper discipline. Both of the defendants' mothers have led dissolute and drunken lives, and one continues to do so. Indeed, when she was visited by police she was in a state of unconscious inebriation. A pathetic drunk, of no use to her family or to society. What an example these women set! Is it any surprise that we find their children before us today guilty of these very grave offences?'

My heart let rip, and I couldn't stop it. Even if I could have, I wouldn't have.

'You can say what you like about me, but don't you dare call my mum a pathetic drunk!'

My anger turned to hot, bitter tears. What does he know about my mum? What does he know about me? What does he know about Reg? What does he know about anything?

'What about Jack the Ripper! What are you doin' about him? You're lettin' him get away with murder!'

The magistrate lifted his arm solemnly and pointed a shaking, crooked finger at me. I had rattled him. He was angry.

'James Hunter. You are in contempt of court. That outburst has cost you another twelve months' imprisonment to run consecutively with a minimum of ten years in prison for the offences of theft and violence . . .'

The dizziness returned and I gripped the spikes again, harder. Eleven years. That was more than I could remember. I couldn't do it. It might as well be a million years.

'You bustard!'

Did I say that out loud? I looked around the court. Yes, I had. Shocked court officials and policemen looked towards the magistrate to see what he would do. The magistrate sat there, staring at me for several seconds. Then his mouth became a no-lipped crack again, except that the corners were turned up. It took a while to realize that he was smiling.

'That makes twelve years. The first twelve years of your manhood. The prime of your life, wasted.'

He pointed his shaking, crooked finger at me again.

'Think on that, young man.'

I stared back at him and concentrated on keeping my mouth clamped shut so tight that my jaw ached.

But my life was over.

Reg got eight years, six for the theft and another two for resisting arrest. He sat there quietly. He didn't have a go at me. He didn't blame me. He just sat there.

Then, after a minute of long silence, the reason for everything became clear. The magistrate shuffled the papers on his desk again.

'But, in this case, I am going to exercise my merciful discretion and implement the special arrangement the court has with the Mayor's recruitment committee. I am sure that the Portsmouth Battalion will offer everything your lives currently lack. Discipline, routine, self-respect and a sense of purpose. It will also give a productive outlet for your obvious aggression. And what greater purpose is there, than to fight for your King and country? Play the man! Make your country proud of you!'

★

The dizziness returned and the coffin became real. The hole was dug. Reg and I were being buried.

A part of me that I thought I'd left behind was saying, we're only fourteen, please, we're only fourteen. Please don't do this. We're too young.

I was half aware of the two coppers who gripped my arms and marched me down the steps from the dock into the darkness of the corridors, out of the court building and into the blinding daylight. Reg followed, flanked by two more coppers. I blinked and adjusted to the light, desperately looking around the busy square for a familiar face, someone who would help. I tried to catch the eyes of people passing by, but nobody met my eye, nobody saw me. I opened my mouth to shout 'Help us!' but nothing came out. Packed trams rattled past, like it was just another day. Office workers walked by with newspapers under their arms. Horse-drawn delivery carts clopped by. Kids skipped on and off the kerb, chanting a rhyme. A newspaper seller shouted his cry on the other side of the square. I couldn't speak. I couldn't be seen. I was lost.

Then I heard a shout.

'Stop! Grab 'im!'

Reg had broken free. My heart leapt.

'Go, Reg, go! Warn Mum! Warn everyone!'

The coppers holding me didn't know whether to join the chase or keep hold of me, so I kicked them to make sure they tightened their grip and wouldn't let go, so as to give Reg a better chance.

'Run, Reg, run!'

Reg dodged through the crowd and was soon lost in the distance, swallowed up by the bustle in Commercial Road. I didn't care that the coppers hit me again. Reg would warn Mum about Jack the Ripper, and word would spread amongst the sisters and all round Portsea.

The recruitment office was in a converted part of the Gas Company offices in the Town Square. It was decked out in recruiting posters and Union Jacks, but in the middle of the wall, in a gold and ornate frame above a desk, was the familiar face of King George. Except this time he had even more medals than before.

The recruiting corporal was a big man with a booming voice and a stick tucked under his arm. He looked at me and raised an eyebrow.

'What 'ave we 'ere?'

The policeman with the moustache handed him a sheet of paper and winked. 'A willing recruit for you, sir. There should have been two, but one of 'em got away.'

The corporal smiled and sized me up.

'A willin' recruit, eh? We likes willin'.'

'We'll catch the other one soon enough.'

The corporal nodded. He reached into his uniform jacket pocket and flicked something at me. I knew what it was instinctively. My hand met it and held it. It's a reflex. It sometimes happens if you're lucky, before the coin reaches the mud.

I opened my hand. It was a silver shilling.

'You 'ave now taken the King's Shilling. That's the

contract signed and sealed, over and done with. You're in the army now, laddie.'

'But . . . you can't do this . . . I'm only fourteen . . . My mum'll be expecting me. I must get back to my mum . . .'

The corporal held up the sheet of paper and tapped it with his stick.

'It says 'ere that you're nineteen, so nineteen is yer hofficial age. Types like you wasn't hofficially registered when you was born, so yer age is decided for you. And cos yer in the army now, you'll find we can do what we bleedin' like. It's no use whinin' fer yer ma, or fightin' yer own war. No. You got to fight fer yer King and country now, laddie. You got to fight the 'Un.'

I glanced over towards the door and weighed up the chances. I'd be faster, that's for sure, but there were two of them. Reg had made it, and I'm faster than him.

The corporal read my thoughts and stepped sideways, blocking my route to the door.

'And don't think you can escape, laddie. Them soldiers what runs away lets everyone down. They is scum. Your mate is lucky. If he'd made a run fer it *after* takin' the King's Shillin' he would be a deserter. And you know what 'appens to deserters?'

I nodded, but he wanted to tell me anyway. He wanted to relish it.

'They gets shot at dawn, laddie.'

Chapter Nineteen

When I was little, Mum used to take me up Portsdown Hill for picnics every year, and the sun always shone a special warm yellow for us. But now it was grey winter, and the sun was nowhere.

I'd been ordered – me, ordered! – to queue up outside the medical officer's tent for a check-up. As the line shuffled along I breathed in deeply. When I was little, the country air drifting up from over the hill had seemed fresher and cleaner than the sea breeze down on the harbour. Instead of salt and ozone it had pollen, wildflower scents and butterflies. But not today. The army blacksmith was shoeing horses and the stench of burnt hooves attacked the inside of my nose.

'What's the matter with you, soldier? Are you blubbin'?'

Sergeant Brough craned his head and studied my face at close quarters.

'Naah, it's that smoke. It's makin' me eyes water,' I lied, wiping away the tears with the sleeve of my new uniform.

Sergeant Brough nodded without saying anything and continued his walk up the line of new recruits.

A day on the hill was our summer holiday, away from the streets of Portsea. We never went any further. The sea to the south and the hill in the north were the two boundaries between Portsmouth and everywhere else in the world.

But the hill was now a training camp for new recruits to Kitchener's Army as well as the thousands of regular soldiers who were waiting to embark for France and fight the Hun. Flapping above our camp, the Portsmouth Chums Battalion flag reminded us who we were. I wasn't about to forget.

For as far as you could see, to the east and the west, hundreds of white bell tents were spotting the slopes, like mushrooms waiting to be picked. Wisps of smoke showed where fires were burning, food was being cooked or horses shod. One day the mushrooms were there, and then they would be gone. Then, overnight, new ones would appear in their place, fresh and ripe.

We didn't sleep much in our tent. The wind off the Solent shook the canvas over and over, billowing and clapping, billowing and clapping, in and out, over and over. There were fifteen of us, and I knew from the sound of stifled crying at night that I wasn't the only one who didn't want to be there. But it wasn't the wind or the cold or anger at being there that kept me awake. It was worrying about Mum. Had Reg managed to get away and warn her about the Ripper?

★

'Move along there!'

I'd let a gap form in the queue in front of me and Sergeant Brough was quick to pounce.

'There's no place for daydreamin' in the army, Private Hunter. Soldiers have to be alert at all times. It could cost you your life or, more importantly, the lives of your comrades.'

'Yeah. Whatever.'

'Private Hunter. You will address a senior officer as "sir" at all times. Understood?'

'Yeah. Whatever. Sir.'

Sergeant Brough stared at me and I stared back.

'I'll let it go this time, Hunter. But next time you'll be on a charge. Understood?'

'Yes.'

He raised an eyebrow.

'Sir.'

This was my new identity. Private Hunter. But there was nothing private about being a soldier. Everything you did was watched, measured and judged. I didn't belong to me any more.

Sergeant Brough was our drill instructor and arms trainer. He had two weeks to knock us into shape. He was about fifty years old, with a square jaw, square shoulders and a disconcerting habit of moving his head in a circle before he spoke. This was to disengage a wart on the back of his neck from his collar. On the first day he caught one of the men mimicking him, and his punishment was to empty the camp latrines for the rest of the week. Nobody ever did it again.

At first the uniform was itchy, heavy and stiff. It felt like I was stuck in a suit of armour that had been invaded by an army of Coliseum fleas. But after a week of drilling it had loosened up and was quite comfortable. But the winter wind was hard and bitter, and the cold cut through to the marrow of our bones, so we looked forward to the twice-daily drill to keep warm. When you're drilling it's like you're not there. You're a machine with pistons. Before, I'd never understood why soldiers marched up and down without going anywhere. And stamped their feet like they had something against the world. It had all seemed pretty pointless to me.

Well, now I know. It's survival. Stop and you freeze up.

The best thing was the boots. Sure, they were heavy at first, but after a few days of drill and marching up and down the hill my feet had moulded themselves to their shape and they become a part of me.

A good pair of boots. This was what Mum wanted for me, and now I had them, for free, courtesy of Lord Kitchener. I needed to let Mum know that I was all right. I needed to tell her that there was no need for her to do what she did, to scrimp and save to look after me any more. I had my boots. I was getting fed. I was all right now. She could do something else for a living, something that didn't put her in danger.

★

'Private Hunter! Pay attention!'

Sergeant Brough was definitely on my back. He was standing over at the other side of the camp with his hands on his hips. His voice carried as clear as the Dockyard whistle. I shuffled forward again to fill the gap.

None of the volunteers in our tent came from Portsea, which didn't surprise me. One thing you learn, growing up in Portsea, you learn to survive, and to survive you never volunteer for anything. You keep your head down and get on with surviving. The men that I'd talked to in my battalion had all volunteered, but I heard rumours of others like me who'd been forced into it because someone, somewhere, had decided that they were troublemakers.

The queue shuffled forward, and this time I kept up. It would only be a few more minutes before it was my turn to be examined. What could I pretend to have that would make me medically unfit? A limp? A weak heart? Madness?

I knew it wouldn't make any difference. Everyone knew that you were passed A1, however bad or mad you were. They wanted men to fight and they didn't care what shape you were in. There was no escape. I had to accept that I was in the army. Nothing was going to change that. All I had to do was make sure that Mum was all right, and that I came back from the war in one piece. Simple as that.

I looked out over Portsmouth. The blacksmith's smoke billowed out gently and was then caught by the wind, carried off and dispersed over the town. In the distance I could see the harbour opening out into the Solent, a silver streak that separated the Isle of Wight from the mainland. And, on the eastern side of the harbour, the Dockyard cranes stood like giant seabirds silently feeding at the water's edge.

That's what us mudlarks were, really, picking titbits out of the mud.

Would I ever smell the fresh, black mud and feel it round my knees again? Or sit in my old tin bath? Or give Reg a dead arm? Or see Pompey play? That smoke was still getting in my eyes, irritating them, making them water.

I could see the tide was out and the railway pier jutting out into the harbour mud. Jop would be folding up copies of the afternoon edition and delivering them into the hands of the dockies finishing the early day shift.

Moored up-harbour was the steam liner where I guessed Mr and Mrs Vosbrugh were imprisoned. I wondered how long they'd be kept there. When the war started, everyone said it would be over by Christmas – but, to be fair, they didn't say which one. Would I bite into a Vosbrugh creamy toffee apple again with Reg and Archie and Lillie? No. Everything was changing and it was hard to see how things could go back to the way they were, even if the war ended tomorrow.

There, between the cranes and the harbour mouth, was Portsea with its narrow, terraced streets. I tried to pinpoint exactly where Jubilee Terrace was, but the parallel lines of slate roofs merged into one grey mass. Somewhere out there, in one of those streets, one of those houses, was Jack the Ripper.

'Get yer b–b–bleedin' 'ands off!'

The cry came from the medical officer's tent. There was a stunned silence in the queue. Then laughter. Word went down the line and the ripple of laughter followed and grew until it seemed like the whole camp was laughing.

Suddenly Sergeant Brough appeared, barking at us to shut up.

That cry, I could have sworn it was Reg.

'Get yer b–b–bleedin' 'ands off me g–g–goolies, yer p–p–pervert!'

The laughter started up again, doubly loud, and Sergeant Brough was powerless to stop us.

The Coliseum was a lifetime ago. This was our way of getting rid of the dirty old men. Me and Reg.

Reg?

It had to be. Had to be.

It was.

Reg was struggling to do up his trousers while being half dragged and half carried out of the tent by two stout orderlies who had been ordered to make sure his feet didn't touch the ground. They gave him a heave, his trousers fell to his ankles and he sprawled on the grass and knocked out two tent pegs as he rolled over. The guy ropes immediately slackened, there was a creaking sound and the tent collapsed in on itself. The whole camp erupted again. Sergeant Brough and the orderlies disappeared under the canvas to rescue the medical officer, whose figure could be seen struggling frantically in the middle, enveloped by the material.

I ran over, laughing.

'Reg!'

I held out my hand to pull him up, but I should have expected the yank on my arm, followed by the headlong flight into the grass beside him. This was Reg, after all.

'Hello, Jimmy, ya b-b-bustard! Did you s-s-see that? I'm gonna s-s-sell that routine to Charlie Chaplin fer 'is next p-p-picture!'

'Reg!'

We pulled ourselves up and brushed off our uniforms.

'You're a sight for sore eyes, Reg!' I punched him on the arm. He was looking well, considering the state he was in the last time I saw him. All that remained from his scrap with Archie was a faint scar over his eyebrow and a gap in his teeth when he smiled. And he was smiling now, from ear to ear.

'You look j-j-just like a b-b-bleedin' s-s-soldier!' laughed Reg, punching me back.

'You shouldn't judge by appearances, Reg. I ain't really a soldier. I'm a mudlark in disguise.' I looked at Reg's uniform. 'Just like you!'

Reg kept his smile, but it became one of those that has worry behind it.

'You and m-m-me, too.'

'Come on, we better make ourselves scarce or we'll be on a charge. Sergeant Brough's a bit of a stickler.'

More soldiers had disappeared under the canvas to

help, and the tent looked like a giant bag of mad ferrets that were frantic to escape. We slipped away and found a hiding place behind the latrine sheds.

'Reg. How's me mum?'

'She's all right. Worried s-s-sick about you, though.'

'But did you tell her about the murders? About Jack the Ripper?'

'Yeah, of c-c-course. She's stopped w-w-working the pubs. And she's s-s-stopped drinking!'

Those were the words I wanted to hear.

'She's spread the w-w-word and some of the s-s-sisters have stopped night-working too. Those that haven't are bein' very c-c-careful, lookin' out fer each other.'

I slowly breathed out my relief. Mum was safe.

'If you weren't so bloody ugly, Reg, I'd give you a great big kiss.'

Reg stepped back, horrified.

'They'd k-k-kick you out the army fer doin' that!'

I smiled.

'If only.'

We both cracked up and laughed for longer than I can ever remember. I realized that my face felt strange and tight. I hadn't laughed for such a long time that my face muscles had almost forgotten what to do.

We watched the blacksmith, further up the hill, repairing the wheel of a gun carriage, the sound of metal on metal filling our ears. The hammer gave the orders and the rivets complied. I looked at Reg. I was sorry that he'd been trapped like me, but it was great to be with him again. I know it was selfish, but I was glad he was here with me. If anyone could make army life bearable, Reg could.

'Yer mum s-s-suspected something was goin' on. She knew Poll hadn't d-d-done herself in.'

'Did she know why they're coverin' it up?'

Reg shook his head. 'She d-d-didn't say. But they can't k-k-keep the lid on this fer long, c-c-can they?'

I shrugged. 'Who knows? The police, the coroner and the court are in on it.'

'So that's the real reason why we're here, is it? Nothin' to do with them coppers' boots, but cos of somethin' to do with Jack the Ripper?'

I nodded. Talking to Reg was helping me to clarify what I knew.

'Yeah. I reckon they didn't want us sniffin' round, askin' any more questions. They were on to us when we talked to that copper and mentioned the whistle code. I reckon five short blasts must mean another victim has been found. They must have kept their eye on us after that. They almost caught me, following the coppers to another murder scene. They said as much to me. My curiosity has caught up with me, they said.'

'What about the b-b-boots?'

'I reckon they were just an excuse to force us into the army. I don't know why they're coverin' up the murders, though. It don't make any sense.'

Reg took off his cap and scratched his head.

'I'm sorry, Reg. I know I talked you into it. It's all my stupid fault.'

'No,' Reg said, replacing his cap, 'it's not your f-f-fault that Jack the f-f-flippin' Ripper's come out of retirement and m-m-moved to Portsea. Do you know how m-m-many victims there 'ave been so far?'

'Seven. That's what I heard.'

'Bloody 'ell. Are they just gonna let 'im c-c-carry on? It's m-m-mad!' Reg put his head in his hands.

I felt his frustration and anger. 'Jop's right. The newspaper is full of lies. They're reporting the murders as suicide and nat'ral causes.'

Reg shook his head. 'But they're only reportin' what the p-p-police tell 'em. I mean, how w-w-would they know any different?'

'P'rhap's Jack the Ripper's a mad c-c-copper. Why else would they c-c-cover it up? Or it c-c-could be s-s-someone really p-p-powerful that they're protecting.'

'What, even more powerful than the police? There ain't anyone, is there? I mean, they are the law, aren't they?'

Reg thought for a minute.

'R-r-rumour 'as it that J-J-Jack the Ripper was an aristo. I remember me ma sayin' that he must 'ave been a nob. Or even royalty.'

'Yeah, I heard that. But nobody really believes it, do they?'

'Naah. What I'm sayin' is that it must be s-s-someone with c-c-clout.'

'So we're lookin' fer someone who's powerful and mad. That narrows it down to every copper, politician and aristo in the world.'

'Yep. That's about the s-s-size of it,' laughed Reg with one of those laughs that doesn't really get started.

I shook my head. 'One thing's for sure. It ain't safe out there. What are we gonna do, Reg? We can't leave it like this.'

Reg frowned, deep in thought. Suddenly his face lit up.

'The n-n-newspaper! We've got to get to the *Portsmouth Times* office and t-t-tell them the s-s-story! They'd kill fer a s-s-story like this.'

Reg was right. An exclusive Jack the Ripper story must be every reporter's dream! With their help, the whole world would soon know that Jack was back, and the police cover-up would be blown apart.

'You're brilliant, Reg! And if we're quick, we could pop in home and say a proper goodbye to our mums.'

The blacksmith's hammer was still busy on the carriage gun. Reg cupped his ear.

'S-s-sorry?'

'I said, you're brilliant, Reg.'

Reg leant over closer. 'No, didn't quite c-c-catch it, Jimmy. Once more?'

I told Reg he was brilliant for the third time, caught his smile, and gave him a dead arm.

Chapter Twenty

A cold, black night. The moon hides behind dark clouds. A furtive, shadowy figure climbs a fence. He jumps down and hides behind a bush.

I could hear the pianist at the Coliseum, thumping out dramatic chords.

Reg stands up and waves his arm. Somehow he manages to shout and whisper at the same time.

'C-c-come on, Jimmy! It's all c-c-clear!'

I must concentrate. The chords playing in my head stop. I find a foothold and push myself up, gripping the wooden fence post at the top, and pull myself over. I join Reg in the bush.

But suddenly an armed Tommy appears and the chords start up again. As he approaches, they change from dramatic to patriotic.

Reg and I duck our heads. I can feel my heart trying to beat its way out of my chest. I swear the guard will hear it. As I crouch there, I realize: we are the enemy. We would have deep, sinister chords.

★

The Tommy puts his rifle down, leaning it against the fence post, and lights up a cigarette. He looks out over Portsmouth. The yellow gas and white electric lights of the town are twinkling like stars that have fallen to earth and clustered together for a party.

He snorts and spits and walks over to the bush. Our bush.

Reg and I instinctively catch our breath before they reach the cold night air and betray us.

The Tommy stands in front of where Reg is and unbuttons his fly.

It's dark, but I catch the look of realization and panic in Reg's eyes.

The Tommy starts to sing with the side of his mouth that doesn't have a cigarette hanging from it.

'It's a long way to Tipperary, it's a long way to go . . .'

He can't sing, but that doesn't stop him.

'It's a long way to Tipperary, to the sweetest girl I know . . .'

A cloud of hot steam rises up from where Reg is crouching.

'Goodbye, Piccadilly, farewell, Leicester Square . . .'

Poor Reg.

'It's a long, long way to Tipperary, but my heart's right there!'

A part of me is thankful that I'm here and Reg is over there. And another part of me, a part of me that I'm not proud of, wants to laugh.

The Tommy grunts, shakes, adjusts and buttons himself

up. He flicks his fag-end towards my part of the bush, and I hear it tumbling through the dense hedge-growth above me.

I watch as the Tommy picks up his rifle and saunters off round the camp perimeter, whistling that it is still a long way to Tipperary.

As the whistling receded I felt a hot, piercing pain on the back of my neck. I screamed into my hand. The cigarette!

I leapt out of the bush. Hot ash was tripping down my back. It stopped at the bottom of my tunic where it bunches up. I ripped off my coat and tunic, popping several buttons off in the process, and jumped up and down on the glowing fag-end, swearing under my breath. I stamped on it, over and over, then ground it into the earth with the heel of my boot.

I heard laughter from the steaming bush.

'If the 'Un could s-s-see you, they'd s-s-surrender immediately, n-n-no question! I'm pretty sure it's d-d-dead, Jimmy!'

Reg climbed out of the bush, still laughing. There he was, steaming like a pudding that's just been put on the kitchen table. And there was me, stripped to the waist, with my teeth chattering like I'm riding a bicycle with no tyres on cobbles. It was like the reels had got mixed up at the Coliseum, and the Charlie Chaplin had been put on by mistake. Except that, to my knowledge, I don't think Charlie has ever been pissed on.

After we'd composed ourselves, I picked up my tunic and coat, and Reg helped me find the buttons in the darkness. Mum would have a needle and thread. We clambered sideways down the hill. Reg deliberately rolled down part of the way in the hope that the wetness would somehow be squeezed out, like in a mangle. That was his theory, anyway, but it didn't work. The dark patch on his shoulder and back remained like a map of somewhere nobody wanted to go.

At the foot of the hill we climbed another fence, found ourselves on the Portsmouth Road and headed south towards the town. There's something about a uniform and boots that makes you march rather than walk. I hadn't been doing drill practice for long, but it was having an effect already.

'Keep up, Reg!' I commanded, in my best Sergeant Brough, military voice.

Then, from behind, we heard the familiar clatter and rumble of a tram and, as it passed, we jumped on the platform. We were lucky, it was a Number 1, headed for Commercial Road, near where the *Portsmouth Times* office was.

The conductor had a jet-black handlebar moustache that was waxed and twisted at each end. He saw our uniforms and smiled. The twisty, waxy points stood up in approval.

I pulled out my silver shilling and offered it to him, but he just patted me on the back.

'You're all right, Tommy lads. I don't see people in uniforms. And if I don't see 'em, I don't charge 'em.'

I smiled and nodded my thanks. I hadn't known the

power of the uniform. Thinking about it, it made me feel taller. Or perhaps it was the boots. And the conductor and passengers on the tram were looking at us with a look I wasn't used to. It took a little while to realize what it was.

Respect.

It made a change from the insults and looks of disgust you got as a mudlark. They say that mud sticks, and it does normally. Take my word for it. But when you're wearing the uniform of the King's Army, different laws apply. A couple of factory girls sitting at the front turned, looked us up and down and smiled. I thought about Maddy. She would never have stood me up if I'd been wearing my khaki. She'd be proud to be seen with me, and she'd show me off to all her friends.

We started to climb the stairs and the conductor went to pat Reg on the back too but he stopped himself when he saw the patch. His nose twitched at the smell, and the twisty, waxy points drooped.

We sat at the front on the top deck and Reg draped his coat over the bar so that the wind would dry it out a bit.

'M-m-me m-m-mum'll kill m-m-me if she sees the state of that.'

'I shouldn't worry, Reg, it ain't yer mum you got to worry about killing you. It's the rest of the world you got to keep yer eye on.'

Reg looked at me. 'Ha b-b-bloody ha.'

He leant back in the seat and closed his eyes. I breathed in the cold night air and stared at the sky. The clouds were moving and the blue moon was starting to shine.

Everything would be all right once the newspaper had the story. The cover-up would be exposed and the police would have to arrest Jack the Ripper, whoever he might be.

I closed my eyes too. I was tired, but the wind in my face made me feel alive. It was one of those moments when you appreciate everything good that you've ever known or had. Like Reg. And my freedom. Tonight I had both.

Tomorrow?

Another day.

Chapter Twenty-one

'I hate to mention it, Reg, but you smell like a public convenience.'

Reg punched me on the arm. He'd put his coat back on, and the heat from his body had made it pong a bit.

'Well, I'd rather b–b–be a t–t–toilet than an a–a–ashtray.'

We turned the corner off Commercial Road. It was a short walk to the office of the *Portsmouth Times*.

'Don't stand in the same place too long, Reg, or you'll have people forming a queue.'

Reg smiled and punched me again. He was trying to think of another reply, but one didn't come. I was going to win this one.

'You'd probably collect more pennies than you get mudlarkin'.'

Reg laughed and punched me again.

'P–p–piss off.'

I looked at his coat. 'Nope, it's still there, Reg.'

This time it was the mother of dead arms. And I deserved it.

★

'W-w-what's that?' asked Reg as we stood on the pavement outside the entrance to the *Portsmouth Times* offices. I could feel it too, through my boots. The pavement was vibrating.

'Dunno, Reg. Feels like a tram's about to go up our arses!'

Reg looked around just in case, but there were no trams about.

We pushed the bell on the door and the elderly night messenger let us in as soon as he saw our uniform.

'Is the editor available?' I asked in my best posh. 'We wish to see him on a matter of some urgency.'

'Mr Ralphs? He'll be in his office.' He opened the door wide and beckoned with his arm. 'Follow me, young sirs.'

The old man shuffled down a corridor, and Reg and I followed. We were led through to a large hall and I realized what was causing the pavement to shake. Two large printing presses filled the hall. They pounded and clattered so loudly that Reg and I instinctively stuck our fingers in our ears.

'That's tomorrow's special casualties supplement,' the old man shouted as Reg and I watched sheets of paper shoot past us blank, go through some rollers, into the press and then return, neatly printed and folded.

We passed two men minding the machines who were pulling copies off at regular intervals to check the print quality. They were both covered in black ink. Reg and I exchanged a smile. They looked like two old mudlarks – Reg and me in fifty years' time.

The noise subsided as we were taken down a long

corridor. Along the walls, large paintings of Portsmouth's mayors and councillors hung on one side and editors of the newspaper on the other, identified by small plaques with the years they were around. Not one of them was smiling.

We reached the end of the corridor and the messenger tapped on a door marked 'MR RALPHS, CHIEF EDITOR'. From behind it came a hacking cough, which eventually turned into the word, 'Come!'

We were admitted into a gloomy, dark-panelled room. Mr Ralphs was sitting in the middle of a cloud of smoke, and a pipe was just visible, jutting out from his face. He waved towards a couple of chairs before looking up from behind his huge desk and studying us for a few seconds until the smoke dispersed and he could see us clearly. He took the pipe from his mouth and smiled broadly.

'Good evening – or should I say "Good morning" – to you both. May I say what a privilege it is to welcome two of our brave defenders to the offices of our humble newspaper!'

He leant forward, coughed into his hand, and then gave Reg and me a moist but firm handshake. Smiling back, I surreptitiously wiped my palm on my army trousers, and I noticed Reg was doing the same.

Mr Ralphs's face beamed with respect. The uniform magic was still working. Fortunately the smell of the pipe smoke was masking the smell of Reg.

'Here at the *Portsmouth Times*, we work twenty-four

hours a day to keep the people informed of our glorious victories! We would do anything to help our brave boys defend our freedom! Be assured, the *Portsmouth Times* is right behind you! Now, what can I do for you?'

'We've got a story for you, Mr Ralphs. An important story. Front-page stuff. An exclusive!'

Mr Ralphs's eyebrows rose and his brow furrowed. 'Really? Something for tomorrow's edition? Eyewitness accounts of your heroic experiences in battle would be extremely welcome!' He looked above our heads and set the headline in the air. 'How our brave Tommies are sending the Hun back to Berlin.'

He looked back at us for our reaction. '. . . Back to Berlin with a flea in his ear and his tail between his legs! That's what the people want!'

Reg and I exchanged glances, but we weren't giving him the reaction he clearly expected.

I cleared my throat. This wasn't going to be easy. 'No. We wanted to tell you about Jack the Ripper . . .'

Mr Ralphs's face dropped. The uniform magic drained away in an instant.

'I don't think there's anything you can tell me about Jack the Ripper. I was a reporter on the *Whitechapel Gazette* at the time.'

'But he's back! And he's killing women here, in Portsea!'

Mr Ralphs stared at me silently for a few seconds and then laughed.

'I'm sorry. There's clearly been some misunderstanding. The *Portsmouth Times* is a respectable newspaper.

We don't do fiction. May I suggest you visit the publisher of one of those penny dreadfuls.'

'No, seriously, Mr Ralphs. It's true. The police know it's Jack the Ripper, he's killed several times already, but they're coverin' it up. We reckon they're protectin' someone important.'

Mr Ralphs shifted back into his seat and folded his arms. 'Listen. If there had been seven murders in Portsea, I would know about it.'

'But the p-p-police are saying that they're s-s-suicides,' Reg explained. 'They're l-l-lyin'. Coverin' it up!'

'No!' Mr Ralphs slapped his hands on his desk. 'This is ridiculous! Jack the Ripper was never caught, but the idea that he's still around is pure fantasy. He's long dead. And the idea that he is roaming around Portsea is simply . . . preposterous!'

His agitation turned into a coughing fit and he pulled a large handkerchief out of his pocket to stifle it.

'B-b-but it was only twenty-five years ago. If he'd been, s-s-say, twenty-five when he d-d-did them m-m-murders in London, now he'd only be . . .' Reg had always struggled with his maths '. . . er, m-m-middle-aged.'

'Reg is right,' I added. 'He'd be about your age.'

Mr Ralphs shook his head. 'This is nonsense!'

There was a knock on the door. It was the night messenger.

'Sorry to disturb you, sir, but there's a problem in the typesetting department that needs your urgent attention.'

Mr Ralphs stood up, clearly annoyed.

'I'll be back shortly. In the meantime you might like to think about what evidence you have for your ludicrous suggestion.'

The door shut behind him. Reg and I looked at each other. We both knew that he was lying. He'd said seven murders without Reg or me mentioning the number.

He knew.

He was involved.

'Quick!' I said, pointing to the wooden filing cabinet behind Mr Ralphs's desk.

Reg leapt out of his seat and pulled open the top drawer.

'W-w-what are w-w-we lookin' for?'

'Anything. Like the man said, we need evidence! Look under "J" for Jack.'

Reg pulled out a file marked 'J' and handed it to me. I flicked through a pile of letters and newspaper cuttings. Nothing.

'How 'bout "M" for murders?'

We opened the second drawer and the 'M' file. There was a murder section, but it was empty.

'"R" for M-M-Mr Ripper?' suggested Reg, clutching at straws.

The 'R' file was bulging with stuff, which raised our hopes, but it was all about railways and roads and religion and royalty. Under royalty there were seven dated press cuttings describing King George's visits to Portsmouth since the war started.

'"R" for rubbish!' I said, slamming the drawer shut.

What else could it be under? 'Come on, Reg, think! He'll be back soon!'

Outside, we could hear the presses thumping, over and over. We probably wouldn't hear him returning.

'What about "S" for s-s-suicides, Jimmy? I know they were m-m-murders, but he might be l-l-lyin' to 'imself as well as to everyone else.'

I grabbed the bottom drawer and pulled out the 'S' file.

'Schools, ships, shops, soldiers, sports, streets . . . suicides!'

I laid out the contents on the desk and we studied them. The first was an official letter from the War Office. I read it out.

'Dear Mr Ralphs, the Prime Minister has asked me to thank you for your assistance during this time of national emergency, and for fulfilling your obligations under DORA . . .'

'Who the f-f-flippin' 'ell is Dora?' interrupted Reg.

I laughed. 'No, it's not a person. I saw it in the paper the other day. It stands for the Defence of the Realm Act.'

Reg nodded as if he knew what I was talking about. I continued reading.

'As you will appreciate, it is imperative that the nation's interests are defended at all costs. If the truth about these murders became public knowledge it would significantly undermine morale and have serious repercussions for the war effort. All agencies have agreed to continue to treat the murders as suicides, and I know we can rely on you to protect the public from the truth.'

'Does that m-m-mean what I think it m-m-means?'

I nodded.

'The cover-up comes right from the top. This is from the Prime bloody Minister!'

Reg held his head in his hands.

'J-J-Jesus.'

I read the rest of the letter. 'It is vital that this delicate handling of the situation continues, especially as victims are now beginning to appear who are drawn from respectable classes. I know we can rely on your loyalty to your King and country. God save the King!'

From the corridor came the sound of a hacking cough, getting louder.

'Quick!'

Reg slammed the cabinet drawers shut while I scooped up the papers on the desk, thrust them down the front of my trousers and quickly pulled my coat across. Mr Ralphs appeared just as we sat back down.

'Now, where were we?'

He sank into his chair.

'Ah, yes. Evidence. Have you any evidence to back up your wild and irresponsible story?'

I shifted in my seat, feeling the papers sticking into my thighs.

'No, Mr Ralphs. We've thought about what you said and we realize you're right. It's a mad idea.'

'T-t-totally m-m-mad!' laughed Reg, nervously. 'I don't know what we were thinking of!'

Mr Ralphs's face relaxed and he relit his pipe with a lucifer.

'So we don't want to waste any more of your valuable time. And we're off to fight in a few days, aren't we, Reg?'

Reg nodded eagerly. 'C-c-can't wait to g-g-get at the 'Un!'

Mr Ralphs stood up and shook our hands even more firmly than before.

'Good luck! The whole country's depending on men like you. If only I was younger! I'd show the Hun a thing or two!'

Another violent, hacking cough started. We could hear it all the way down the corridor as the messenger led us out. As we left, the presses were still thumping out the casualties supplement. We could feel them as we made our way down the road towards Portsea.

'What did that letter m-m-mean, Jimmy? That bit about victims from the respectable c-c-classes?'

'It means, Reg . . . It means that nobody is safe.'

Chapter Twenty-two

The Nelson pub smelt its familiar smell of stale beer, but the lights were out and the last drinker had long gone. Reg and I figured we would just have enough time to go home, provided we didn't stay too long and got back to camp by six.

We turned into Jubilee Terrace. Such a lot had happened since I was last at home. It felt like I'd been away for years, fighting a war.

I looked across to my house, and my heart leapt and then sank.

The flag was up.

She was all right.

But she had company. Another soldier or sailor from a pub. She must be still working. She must be back on the drink.

I was angry. I pointed at the flag and shouted at Reg. 'I thought you said you'd warned her! She's still doing it! She's still ruddy well doing it!'

Reg looked at the flag. 'I d–d–did tell 'er, Jimmy. Honest. She s–s–said she was g–g–givin' up.'

I sat down on the kerb outside. Nothing had changed. Reg sat down beside me.

I looked at my shiny black boots in the gutter. The polished leather caught the light from the corner lamppost.

I was relieved that Mum was all right, but angry with her at the same time for still putting herself at risk. I couldn't believe it. With Jack the Ripper roaming the streets! There was no need for it. She didn't have to look after me any more. She didn't need to work the pubs.

I calmed down. It wasn't Reg's fault.

'Sorry. I didn't mean to 'ave a go at you, Reg. I'm all right now. You go and see yer ma.'

'No, Jimmy, I d-d-don't m-m-mind s-s-stayin'.'

I could tell he was itching to go, but he was being a mate.

'No, Reg, really. We ain't got long. We got to be back before reveille or we're in deep. Real deep. You go.'

'You s-s-sure, Jimmy?'

'Yeah, Reg.'

Reg stood up and started to cross the road to his house.

'Reg.'

He turned.

'Y-y-yes, Jimmy?'

'Thanks, mate.'

Reg smiled and nodded.

Half a dozen dockies ticked by on their bicycles. The early night shift had just ended. I studied my boots.

The slightest movement changed the light patterns reflected by the folds and surfaces of polished leather, and if you looked into the highlights you could see the lamppost.

The flag was still there. Mum's friends didn't usually stay this long.

There was a movement in the corner of my eye. On the other side of the road a rat bounced along in the gutter. It stopped, stood up on its back legs and stared at me. Its tail twisted and writhed like an exposed lugworm. I thought about what Jop had said about rats. Soldiers' souls, he said. The rat cleaned his whiskers, staring at me all the time, tilting his head from side to side. As he wiped and groomed, his eyes didn't leave me. I guess he was wondering what I was doing, sitting with my feet in the gutter. His gutter, his territory. A door at the end of the street slammed, startling him. His head turned and he looked for safety in the opposite direction, and his body and tail swiftly followed.

The flag was still there. I was starting to worry. Imagination can be a terrible thing when you mix it up with worry.

No. She was all right. Everything would be all right.

But the thought was there and nothing would make it go away. I stood up. My legs ached from where I'd been sitting in the same position for so long.

I walked down the alley to see if there were any lights on round the back. I turned the latch on the back gate and stepped into the yard. A light was coming through from the kitchen, but no sound.

I opened the back door.

'Mum? Are you all right? Mum?'

Mum was slumped over the kitchen table. My heart was pounding. I'd been here before. She'd be all right. She had to be all right.

'Mum?'

She'd be asleep. I went over to her and put my hand on her shoulder and squeezed it gently.

'Mum?'

She raised her head from her arms and looked at me. I breathed out my relief. It took a few seconds for her to wake up properly and recognize me, and in those few seconds she looked terrified. But her terror quickly turned to disbelief and joy.

'Jimmy? Jimmy!'

She stood up and flung her arms round me. She was all right. Everything would be all right. I breathed in deeply. It was the Mum smell. No gin. Just Mum.

'How are ya, Jimmy?'

'I'm fine, Mum.'

'Oh, Jimmy! Let's 'ave a look at yer.'

She held me at arm's length and looked me up and down.

'My! Don't you look the soldier!'

Her face was beaming.

She went on, 'Reg explained what happened. I thought about it fer a long time. I was bloody angry, I can tell you. Bloody angry at the police. And bloody angry at

174

you fer bein' so bloody stupid. Stealin' policemen's boots! That's the most stupidest thing I've ever heard in my life, Jimmy Hunter!'

She waved her finger at me like I was a little boy. I don't know which of us smiled first, but it cracked us both up. We laughed until there were tears in our eyes, and she hugged me so tight it took my breath away.

'I couldn't get you out. I did me best, but no one would listen. The police said it was fer yer own good. They said that the war would be over by Christmas, and that you'd come home a hero, but that if you'd gone to prison I wouldn't see you fer years and you'd come 'ome in disgrace.'

She held me again at arm's length.

'Now, I'm so proud of you. I thought I'd never see you again. I thought you'd never forgive me fer not tellin' you about yer dad."

She was proud of me?

Her face beamed approval. She wasn't just happy to see me, she looked over the moon and far away. She looked so proud, so very proud of me.

'Thanks, Mum. It's good to be home.'

Mum smiled, rolled up her sleeves, put on the kettle and got some bread and dripping out of the larder. She placed the loaf on the breadboard and started sawing with the breadknife.

'You were right, Jimmy. I should have told you about yer dad. That's the biggest regret of me life, and if there was anythin' I could do to put it right, I would.'

As she smeared the dripping on with the knife I could see the water in her eyes. She closed them, sending the tears rolling down her face.

'It's all right, Mum. I'm sorry that I didn't know 'im, but it's important to me that you really loved him and that I was the result. Somehow, it means that I mean somethin'. It means I am somebody.'

I hadn't explained it very well, but Mum nodded and smiled and put the plate down in front of me.

'Get that down ya, Jimmy.'

We sat down at the table and Mum looked into my eyes. I tucked in. The dripping was salty and meaty and the bread thick, just the way I like it.

'I'm pleased that you ain't doin' the mudlarkin' any more. It brought in a few bob, but there weren't no future in it. Now look at you!'

She studied my uniform, feeling the material between her first finger and thumb and rubbing it, then bending down to press the boot leather. And for the first time there was an edge to her voice, a bitterness, something I'd never heard before.

'That's quality. I could never afford that. Not in a lifetime.'

I didn't know what to say. It wasn't like Mum to be bitter. At least, it wasn't like Mum to show it.

She watched me eating.

'How's army grub?'

I had to admit. 'Grub's good, Mum.'

She nodded her approval.

I took another bite and smiled. 'But not as good as yours.'

'I always did me best fer yer. But they're lookin' after you now, son. It's fer the best.'

Her bottom lip and chin quivered for a brief moment, but she turned it into a smile. Another proud smile.

It was all falling into place. She didn't like me mudlarking. Sure, the money helped out, but it was begging. Asking strangers for money? That was begging. Nothing more, nothing less. Cut the crap, Jimmy. You're a beggar. A dirty beggar. And a miserable scavenger. Like the seagulls round the harbour sewer pipe. How could I be so stupid? How could she be proud of a son who begged and scavenged for a living? How could Maddy have gone out with me? How could I imagine that she would fancy me? And how could I be so stupid? Stupid. Stupid. Stupid.

But then I thought, what about what Mum did?

But then I thought, she's always done it because she has to, to look after me.

But not any more. Everything had changed. She was proud of me but she wasn't responsible for me now. We wouldn't be the same with each other ever again. She was still my mum. Nobody could replace her. But now the army was feeding and clothing me and putting boots on my feet. I felt her shame that she'd never been able to do all of that for me.

Mum poured out the tea. She looked again at my uniform and frowned.

'You got a few buttons off there, Jimmy. Give it 'ere and I'll sew 'em back on for yer.'

I pulled the buttons out of my pocket and she fetched a needle and thread from the drawer. She was still my mum.

She put the thread in her mouth to wet it, twisted it into a point between her fingers and guided it, first time, through the eye. Then her elbow went in and out, stitching and pulling, stitching and pulling. I put the words together in my head. She tested the button to make sure it was secure, then bit through the thread. Now was the time.

'Mum. You're not still drinking, are you?'

She twisted the end of the thread into a point and aimed for the eye. Her hand was trembling and she missed. Again. And then again. It was the first time we'd ever mentioned it. The first time I'd ever brought it up with her.

She gave up, put the needle and thread down, and looked at me.

Chapter Twenty-three

'No. I'm not . . . not doing that any more. And I'm never goin' back to it.'

'That's . . . you don't know how happy that makes me. I'm proud of you, Mum.'

I got up and gave her a big hug.

'Mind me tea, ya soppy 'aporth!'

'I'm so proud of you, Mum!'

Mum went all embarrassed.

'So you should be. I've got a job down Hartley's, the naval tailors. Money's not good, but I can just get by cos of all the men what's leavin' fer the war, they're 'avin' to take on women to replace 'em. It's 'appening everywhere. Who'd 'ave thought!'

They say every cloud. Women like Mum were starting to do jobs they'd never been allowed to do before.

I sat back down and sipped my tea. It was hot and sweet, just the way I like it.

'My mum, a tailor!' I laughed and shook my head.

'Well, I'm a pattern-cutter, really. I prepares the cloth for the assemblers. It ain't nearly so grand.'

She threaded the needle and started on another button

and she kept looking at me as she pulled the thread.

'My son, a soldier!'

'Yeah, me a soldier.'

I heard myself sounding unconvinced. Despite the orders and the drilling and the uniform, I couldn't believe it. I felt a fraud, not just because I didn't volunteer, but because I was still me: a kid who happened to be taller than he used to be. A mudlark in a uniform.

Mum's arm swooped in and out, stitching and pulling, stitching and pulling.

'You know, what Reg told me confirmed what I already thought. Two sisters died before poor Poll. But it was Poll's murder that settled it for me. I knew Poll better than anyone. She'd never top 'erself. Not in a million years. I knew it was murder. Knew it. But nobody wanted to know. I went to the police weeks ago, but they ignored me, and when I kept on they threatened to lock me up.'

I recognized Mum's look of desperation. I'd seen it before, in the mirror, just before she pulled down the veil and went to Poll's funeral.

'Then, the other night, there was this bloomin' great bang on the door. I'd never 'eard knocking like that in me life. Frightened the life out of me, I can tell yer. I thought he were goin' to knock a hole in it, he knocked that hard. I got the bread knife ready, just in case. Then I opened the door, ready to 'ave a go.'

'Chrissakes, Mum. That was . . .'

I was searching for a word somewhere between brave and stupid, but I couldn't find one.

'And there was this funny old codger standin' there. Coughin' an' wheezin' like nobody's business, he was. About to take another swing at the door. With 'is wooden leg.'

'Jop? He's been round 'ere?'

I didn't know Jop knew where I lived. I had that strange feeling you get when two very separate parts of your world come together. Like seeing Pompey's centre forward, the best player in the world, chucking up into the gutter outside the Lord Nelson. Or seeing your old headmaster drunk and singing, arm-in-arm with one of the sisters. It takes a few seconds to adjust, to explain it to yourself.

'Yeah, Jop, that's the feller. Said he was a friend of yours. Told me about all the murders. Said the police is coverin' it all up.'

Jop was pretty smart. Not much got past him. What had he discovered about Jack the Ripper? I was willing Mum to get on with it.

'Yeah, Jop was worried cos he 'adn't seen you mudlarkin' fer a while. He came to say goodbye.'

'Goodbye? Where was he going?'

Mum looked surprised, as if I should already know.

'Well, I thought he wanted to say goodbye before you left fer the war, but then it was obvious he didn't know nuffin' about you bein' forced into the army. He was surprised when I told 'im. Then he was angry.'

'Did Jop tell you why the police were coverin' up? Did he know who Jack the Ripper is?'

Mum looked away, closed her eyes and shook her head.

'No. He just seemed . . . like, I don't know, ashamed.'

The kitchen tap dripped noisily. Mum was thinking. She picked up her mug and held it in her hands, feeling the warmth. I don't know why, but I felt she was keeping something back.

She shrugged a shrug of surrender.

'There's no point thinkin' 'bout it. No point.'

The shrug said more. It meant she was powerless to do anything and that it was useless trying. Nothing she could do would change anything or stop the killings. It was a fact of life and one that she had to live with. These things happen. The murders would go on.

All that in one shrug.

It made me angry and frightened.

'I've been spreadin' the word, and a few of the other sisters 'ave given up goin' out at night too. Some of the others are carryin' on but they're keepin' an eye on each other. But there's lots who ain't interested. They reckon it's either worth the risk or they reckon it'll never 'appen to them.'

I explained to Mum what we had discovered that night, and that it could happen to anyone. I could feel the wedge of papers stuck down my belt. There was no time to study them now. That would have to wait until tomorrow.

'Oh, Jimmy. I nearly forgot. As he left, Jop gave these to me. He said I was to take 'em to Berlusconi's and sell 'em, to tide me over. Said he 'ad no more use fer 'em.' Said he was ashamed of his King and country.'

Mum opened the kitchen drawer, pulled out a small

cardboard box and handed it to me. I opened the lid and saw Jop's medals lined up, neat and polished, cushioned in tissue paper.

'I said I couldn't accept 'em, but 'e wouldn't 'ave it. He said he wouldn't be seen dead wearin' 'em. Said he used to spit on 'em to polish 'em up, but now all he wanted to do was just spit on 'em. Said that if I didn't want 'em, I could chuck 'em down the bog.'

'But Jop was very proud of these.' I touched them one by one. I remembered them dancing on his chest when he laughed. That's where they belonged, not hidden in a box in a drawer or up for sale in a pawnbroker's. 'Why was he ashamed of them all of a sudden?'

'Who knows? But 'e also said he wanted to leave you a message. But it don't make any sense. He just said to tell you "trouble".'

'Trouble? What? Nothing else?'

'Well, he said it twice. Like he was making sure I 'eard 'im. Trouble trouble, he said. He reckoned you'd under-stand. By this time he was coughin' and breathin' so bad I told him to get 'imself 'ome to bed with a tonic.'

'Trouble trouble,' I repeated.

I remembered his motto, the saying that he'd sworn by. Don't trouble trouble unless trouble troubles you, he'd said. Well, Reg and I had certainly been troubled by trouble. And the murders had gone on. I reckoned Jop wanted us to do something to stop Jack the Ripper. But what?

There was a gentle tap at the front door.

'That'll be Reg. I've got to go now, Mum. We've got to get back before they discover we're awol. Sergeant Brough'll have us shot or somethin'.'

Mum bit off the cotton and laughed. 'I don't think so. They needs all the soldiers they can get!'

I pulled on my tunic and coat and gave Mum a kiss.

'Bye, Mum. Look after yourself.'

Mum did up my buttons, one by one, just like when I was little. That was always the routine just before going to school: kiss, then buttons, then hug, then, 'Wrap up well,' and finally, 'Don't talk to strangers.'

She gave me the hug.

'You look after yourself, Jimmy. Take care.'

I smiled at the familiar routine. 'And wrap up well?'

She laughed and tears appeared in her eyes.

'Don't . . .'

'Talk to strangers?'

'Yeah, that's right. Just shoot 'em and come 'ome. Specially the last bit.'

Reg didn't say anything. Before we turned the corner I looked back at my house.

My home.

Mum was at the window, waving, with her hand over her mouth. She didn't want me to see her crying.

Below her, the flag was still up.

But this time it was for me.

Chapter Twenty-four

Reg slapped me on the back and then held out his hand when I told him my news.

I looked at it suspiciously, for a second not knowing what I was supposed to do. Then I realized it wasn't a trick. I wasn't about to be thrown headlong into any mud. His hand was open and waiting. I grabbed it.

We shook hands.

Big deal? Well, yes. You see, this was my first ever handshake with Reg. He gripped my hand hard. I felt awkward at first. I mean, it's a pretty silly thing to do really, when you think about it, shaking hands. But then, when we were doing it, it felt as natural as giving him a dead arm.

Reg knew what I'd been through, he knew what it was like. His ma had been beaten up when she was working the pubs. That's what made her give it up and go and work for next to nothing in the corset factory. I guess, at the back of my mind I'd envied him that. But now we were the same, and I felt closer to him than ever. True friends have to go through similar stuff, otherwise there's no true understanding. Not really.

'Mum's safe now,' I said to myself, over and again until I believed it. 'Mum's safe now.' But it wasn't enough. Jop's words stuck with me. Trouble trouble. Jop wanted us to try to stop the murders. Reg agreed that that's what Jop meant, and that it was the right thing to do. But surely it was too late to do anything?

'It don't make sense,' I reasoned, thinking out loud. 'Here we are, goin' off to bleedin' Belgium to fight a bunch of people who we've never met and who 'aven't done us any 'arm as far as I know, while somebody is goin' round our 'ome town, killin' our own!'

'No,' Reg agreed, 'it ain't r-r-right. We're walkin' away, like c-c-cowards.'

'Yeah,' I laughed bitterly. 'Cowards going off to war.'

The last tram had long gone. We'd walked about three miles into town and I could tell from the silence that Reg was still thinking. I knew Reg better than anyone. He usually knew instinctively the right thing to do, but now he was struggling. I could see it in his face.

'I'll go along with anything you want to do, Reg.'

'I don't know w-w-what to do, Jimmy. It's complicated. Besides, me m-m-ma wanted me to s-s-stay. She b-b-begged m-m-me to s-s-stay. We ought to s-s-stay. But . . .' His voice was as flat as mud.

I told him what he already knew. 'They'd only come and fetch us.'

'I know. That's w-w-what I t-t-told 'er.'

'I don't wanna do this, Reg, but the way I see it, there's no way out. They've got us, good and proper. If we don't go, we'll be locked up fer years. And we won't be able to track down Jack the Ripper, not while we're rottin' in prison. But, if we do go, we . . . well, at least this way we've got a fightin' chance. Specially if the war's over soon.'

Reg nodded doubtfully. I didn't believe it either. But you never know.

'Come on, Reg, mate. Me and you. Together.'

I held out my hand and we shook.

'Yeah. You're r-r-right. People would think we're c-c-conchy pacifist puffs if we didn't go.'

His voice was still flat, so I punched him with just-below-dead-arm force. He swung round and got me back with double-dead-arm force.

'No, Reg,' I said, nursing my arm, 'there's no danger of you turnin' into a conchy pacifist puff.'

Away from Portsea, the town was asleep and the only noise was the hum of lampposts which became fewer and further between as we went north, until there were no pavements. Then we walked between the luminous, moonlit silver tramlines that cut cleanly through the granite setts in the middle of the road.

Up ahead, Portsdown Hill loomed wide and large, like a black tidal wave threatening to break and crush and wash the town clean away. We left the road, scaled the fence and climbed the hill up to our camp. Light and shadows started pushing each other, but light was winning. The sun began to rise over Portsmouth.

Reg and I stood and watched the light fill in the detail

of the town. There was a short time, a moment between dark and light, between sleep and awake, when the town looked totally different: a strange, eerie place with long, shifting shadows, where those familiar landmarks – the Town Hall clock tower, the weathervane of St Thomas's, the Dockyard cranes – looked unfamiliar, didn't register, didn't mean anything. You could lose yourself in a town like that.

Looking down, I realized that Portsea was just one place in one town, and that, on the other side of the hill, and on the other side of the sea, there were other places, other towns and cities and countries. Portsea and Portsmouth was all and everything I knew. I'd read and heard about other places but, because I hadn't been to them, they weren't really real to me. They were just words or ideas like the King, or the North Pole or Mars or God.

There was a great, real world out there.

And a great, real war.

The sun cleared the horizon and Portsmouth emerged, like the mud from the tide, renewed, refreshed, ready for a new day.

'I'm knackered. T–t–totally knackered.' Reg bent down wearily and put his hands on his knees.

'Me, too. One more fence to climb.'

'Just r–r–remember it's your turn to get p–p–pissed on.'

I kept lookout while Reg crawled from bush to bush and reached his tent, then I slipped into mine, treading carefully between the sleeping bodies until I reached my space. I pulled the papers out of my trousers and stuffed them in my kitbag to look at later. I undressed wearily and lay down, pulling the blanket up to my eyes, and, the instant I closed them, reveille sounded. The men groaned and stirred and stretched. It was time for ablutions and uniform and kit inspection. But I really didn't mind. I reckon you get to a certain level of tiredness where you feel able to cope with anything, and as I got up I felt like I could take on the world.

Chapter Twenty-five

Lord Kitchener may have given us some nice boots (not personally, you understand), but he didn't have enough rifles to go around, so we had to use mop handles to practise with.

'S-s-still, I s-s-suppose we could k-k-kick 'em to death,' Reg whispered out of the side of his mouth. Sergeant Brough shot us a glance. I had a distinct feeling he was keeping an eye on us.

He looked self-conscious as he handed the mops out, like a supervisory domestic organizing a team of cleaners after a very large spillage. He stood on the mop head with the handle between his legs and demonstrated how to yank and twist it to get it out. This done, he collected the heads up, like a Red Indian chief collecting scalps after a particularly successful massacre.

He then brushed off his uniform, moved his head in a circle, and cleared his throat. 'Now pay attention, men. This is a temporary measure. Generally speaking, imagination isn't something the army likes to encourage in fighting men, but it is a quality I am encouraging today.'

He held up a mop handle. For a brief moment I

thought he was struggling to keep himself from smiling. Perhaps he felt as ridiculous as he looked.

I whispered to Reg, 'Did you see that?'

'W–w–what?'

Perhaps I was wrong. 'Nothing.'

Sergeant Brough shot us another glance before continuing. 'Now, I want you to imagine this is a Lee-Enfield rifle. With its bayonet, it is five foot two inches long and weighs the same as a newborn baby. From today you are new fathers and I would like to take this opportunity to congratulate you all personally. And I would also like to point out to you that it is your responsibility to look after your weapon like it is a newborn baby. Any questions?'

There were no questions, just murmurs of disappointment and dismay as the lads studied their mop handles. Holding it reminded me of when we were little kids, using Dockyard driftwood as guns in the harbour mud. Pretend guns for the boys, or carved baby dolls for the girls. Now we had to treat our pretend guns like pretend babies. It was very confusing.

'P-p-permission to s-s-speak, s-s-sir.'

'Yes, private. What is it?'

Reg had his innocent look on, with his eyebrows raised. 'Sir, I've 'eard a r-r-rumour that the 'Un 'as real g-g-guns.'

There was the tortured sound along the line of giggles and laughs being strangled at birth. I saw a hint of a smile on Sergeant Brough's face for a brief second before it reverted immediately and he shouted at us to be silent.

'I assure you, this is temporary. Now, where was I? Yes, you have to clean your gun and feed it grease regularly. Otherwise it could seize up and cost you your life. And remember. Losing your gun is a serious offence. Field punishment twenty-five-b states that if you cast away your arms, the maximum punishment is death. Any questions?'

Reg cleared his throat again. 'Is that d-d-death by f-f-firing squad, sir?'

Sergeant Brough nodded.

'That'll be a f-f-firing squad of m-m-mop handles, would it, sir?'

Again, a flash of a smile before the threat, 'Don't push it, private.'

Next was target practice. We aimed our mops at the church spires sticking up out of Portsmouth, and Sergeant Brough told us to gently squeeze the imaginary trigger and shout 'Bang'. Reg and I went one better by making exploding noises and pretending to be thrown by the kick-back. Sergeant Brough said this was a good idea and encouraged all the men to do it, and they enjoyed it as much as we did. They were just like us, really.

I took a shot at the Town Hall clock tower, but, as my mouth exploded and I threw myself back, I felt a sharp pain in my hand and dropped my gun.

'I've gone and got a bleedin' splinter from mine.'

I sucked my finger and held it up to inspect. I could see the brown shard just under the skin and I tried to ease it out but it wouldn't budge.

'That's typical, that is. Our weapons are 'armless to everyone except ourselves.'

Sergeant Brough barked back, 'If you don't button your lip, private, I'll stick your mop handle where it will not be visible.'

But then he winked. I was starting to warm to Sergeant Brough. I reckoned he was doing what teachers used to do at school, start off mean and hard and then gradually ease off.

Later that day, and after the fifth time of marching up and down the hill with our mop handles resting on our shoulders, Reg was getting tired and fed up. We all were, but it was Reg who said it.

'S-S-Sergeant Brough reckons he's the Grand Old D-D-Duke of bleedin' York.'

I laughed.

'What was that, private?'

Sergeant Brough was standing right behind us. He pulled us both out of the line by the collar and ordered the rest of the company to carry on.

'You two. Stand to attention when a superior officer addresses you.'

Reg and I stood to attention. He leant forward, his glowering face inches from ours. His teeth were clenched, his jaw stuck out. Perhaps I'd been wrong about him. He stopped in front of Reg, their noses almost touching.

'Now, what was that you said, private?'

'N-n-nothing, s-s-sir.'

There was a long silence. A painfully long silence. I had

to help Reg out, or he'd end up cleaning out the bogs.

'Reg was just saying that your training methods are similar to those of that great military tactician, the Duke of York, sir.'

Sergeant Brough turned to me and his eyes stared deep into mine, searching, probing.

Suddenly they came to life with creases at the sides. His breathing burst, making me and Reg jump, and it turned into laughter, loud and deep. Reg was biting his bottom lip.

'P-p-permission to c-c-crack up too, s-s-sir?'

'Permission granted, soldier!'

We laughed more than we should, long and loud. I'm sure they could hear us on the Isle of Wight.

After that, things were very different with Sarge. It was no more 'sirs' after that. And we never cheeked him again, at least not in front of the men. That night he invited us to his tent and he filled it with pipe smoke and stories from his time in India and in South Africa during the Boer War. And Reg and I told him all about the finer skills of mudlarking, about the angles of elevation of throws, the varying ranges achieved by different coins, and of the fight to get there first before it was swallowed by the black mud.

Sarge listened intently, sucking on his pipe. 'You know, you both remind me of myself when I was a lad, picking coal out the slag heaps.'

He looked at Reg.

'A cheeky pain in the arse,' and then he turned to me, 'and a rebellious pain in the arse!'

We laughed.

'It never goes away, you know,' he said with a pain-in-the-arse twinkle in his eye. 'You just have to hide it as you get older. Specially in the army.'

We laughed again. We were the pain-in-the-arse club. And proud of it.

Sarge tapped the bowl of his pipe on the heel of his boot, scraped out some black ash, stuffed it with more moist brown tobacco from his pouch and struck a lucifer. There was something comfortable and reassuring about the routine and the smell of that pipe smoke.

'Why did you join the army, S–S–Sarge?'

'Didn't have much choice, lad. Where I come from there were two choices. Down the mine or join up. I figured I'd rather take my chances above ground than be buried alive. What's more to the point, what are you two doing here? You're not old enough to shave, let alone fight! What's going on?'

We told him our stories, about the murders and the police and the cover-up, and how we had been forced into the army. He nodded seriously and sucked his pipe. I don't know whether he believed us, but he didn't seem surprised.

'Jack the Ripper's out there, Sarge, but there's nothin' we can do about it. Is there anything you can do? Anybody you can tell?'

He thought for a minute, using his pipe to help him concentrate. His brow furrowed hard and deep with effort, but eventually he shook his head, muttering his frustration with himself.

'No, lads. I'm sorry. As far as I can see, it goes too far up. There's nothing the likes of you or I could do. I'm sorry.'

Reg and I went back to our tents. It was getting late and we didn't feel like talking any more. Sergeant Brough had been our last hope.

One of the men in my tent was playing a harmonica, others were smoking and reading. I lay down on my blanket and remembered the papers from the editor's office. I pulled them out of my haversack, but as I did so the shout went up for 'Lights out'. The oil lamps were extinguished, one by one. The papers would have to wait for tomorrow evening.

Chapter Twenty-six

'Rest assured, men, we will be getting our Lee-Enfields tomorrow. They may not have arrived in time for your training, but they will be here for the visit of our Commander-in-Chief, his majesty King George, who, I have just been informed, will be visiting the hill encampments tomorrow, prior to your embarkation for France in three days' time. And, in keeping with the tradition of royal visits, four hours' leave is granted to all men.'

Sergeant Brough waited for the men's cheers to subside.

'When you are ordered to present arms and salute your King, you will be able to do so fully kitted out, with pride and honour as befitting such an auspicious occasion.'

The men cheered again. We would be real soldiers soon, with real guns. And while Reg and I weren't exactly what you might call monarchists, we agreed that it would be interesting to see the King in the flesh. I could chat to him about how he came by all his medals.

It was hard to believe that the Portsmouth Chums were now, officially, fully trained soldiers, ready to fight for our

King and country. We knew how to salute and drill, put up a tent and fire a gun (in theory). But that was about it.

It wasn't Sarge's fault. He'd done his best, with the equipment he had, following the orders he had. He was a good actor, covering up what he really thought about things. Reg and I were the only ones who knew what he was really like. When he was addressing the battalion, it was like a private joke that only the two of us were in on.

That night, in his tent, he told us things about being a soldier that weren't in any manual. The first rule in the soldier's unwritten code was that you never tell people back home what you did in the war. You never tell them what it's really like. But, because we were fellow soldiers, he could describe to us what he'd seen in the Boer War. He told us about the concentration camps that Lord Kitchener set up in South Africa, and what British soldiers did to the women and children there. It was terrible, but I can't go into details. Because of his experiences, he had nothing but scorn for his superiors, and that included the way they were running this war.

'Between you and me,' he confided, 'they couldn't organize a piss in a pot. Those that don't wet their pants, wet their boots.'

'What, even the King?' I imagined the King pissing on his royal boots.

'No, lad, he's just a figurehead. All he does is wear the uniform. He doesn't have anything to do with the war, even though officially he's our Commander-in-Chief. He just comes down here to cheer up the troops. Tomorrow will be the eighth battalion he's seen off from Portsmouth.

He's become quite a regular visitor to these parts, has His Majesty.'

'Eight?' I was surprised. But then I remembered the press cuttings we'd seen in the editor's office under 'R' for royalty.

'Still, I expect he needs a b-b-break, what with all that strenuous p-p-posin' for postage stamps,' said Reg. 'W-w-will he talk to us, Sarge?'

Reg knew it was a daft question the moment he asked.

'No, lad, he doesn't talk to the likes of you and me. He only talks to very senior officers.'

'What would you say to His Maj if you got the chance, Reg?'

Reg thought for a few seconds. 'I'd c-c-call 'im daddy and g-g-give 'im a hug. Did I ever t-t-tell you that he's got a bit of a sp-sp-speech impediment and that one of the p-p-princes has got a bad stammer too? Runs in the family. So it's odds on that he's me real d-d-da.'

I smiled. Reg had been keeping this joke fantasy going for ages without let-up.

Sergeant Brough laughed. 'So the real reason King George keeps visiting Portsmouth is not to boost morale, but to search for his long-lost son!'

'You've 'it the n-n-nail on the 'ead, Sarge.'

'More like the fingers 'olding it,' I added.

Sergeant Brough tamped down some springy fresh tobacco with his thumb, struck a lucifer on his boot and stoked up another pipe.

''Fraid it'll be time for lights out soon, lads.'

We didn't want to go, but we knew it had to end. This

was our second-to-last night together. The three of us, talking and laughing. Us against the world. The pain-in-the-arse club. Tomorrow the King would visit and then, at the end of the week, we'd be put on a troopship and sent to fight. For King and country.

Back in my tent, I pulled out the papers and held them close to the oil lamp that hung from the tent post. I had a few minutes before lights out. I read every one. I re-read the letter about the cover-up. I read the press cuttings that had appeared, reporting the so-called suicides. And then I came across a list. It was a list of the victims, giving their names and the estimated dates of death. It was when I got to the end of the list that I knew.

I knew.

It hit me in the gut and the head.

I felt winded and sick.

I'd belly-flopped off the pier.

But the tide was out.

I got out Maddy's thruppenny piece and held it in my hand. I squeezed it and closed my eyes tightly until the tears came.

The camp buzzed with excitement as our equipment arrived the next morning. I was not buzzing. I was not excited. I was angry.

At ablutions I washed away the stickiness of the dried tears from my face. But the anger stayed.

The crates were unpacked and we queued for our

Lee-Enfields. I held mine in my hands. This was my baby. It felt good. Heavy and powerful. I was starting to believe that I was a soldier.

The next line was for bayonets.

They were sharp and long.

One foot six inches long.

As long as my forearm.

Long.

We practised fixing it on and taking it off.

'W-w-where's the instructions for actually using it?' asked Reg, looking around for a leaflet.

The men laughed nervously.

Reg smiled at me. 'You all right, J-J-Jimmy? You're very q-q-quiet this morning.'

'Yeah, Reg. I'll explain later. Not here. Not now.'

We queued for the ammunition. We were counted out twelve rounds each. They were cold and heavy. Sergeant Brough showed us how to load the rifle.

Holding a rifle that's loaded changes you. It's got something to do with power. Reg felt it too.

'M-m-makes ya think, don't it?' Reg was holding his awkwardly, at arm's length.

'You took the words right out of my . . .'

'M-m-mouth?'

'Yeah,' I breathed. I felt as if I had the answer to every problem in my hands.

'The army must be b-b-barmy, handing these things out. S-s-someone could get s-s-seriously hurt.'

Reg smiled, but I didn't return it. I had to tell him

what was on my mind. I had to tell him what I knew. Time was running out and I suddenly felt a rush of panic. We'd be sent to France in a couple of days.

'W-w-what's up, Jimmy? All morning you've looked like you p-p-pooped yer pants and f-f-found the laundry's shut.'

It couldn't wait. I put my arm around Reg's shoulder and walked him away from the men.

I whispered in his ear. 'Reg. Listen to me. Maddy's dead!'

Reg looked me straight in the eyes. 'M-M-Maddy?!'

'Yes.'

'D-d-dead?'

'Yes.'

'B-b-but how?'

'Murdered. Like all the others. The bustard's killing girls who are out alone in Portsea at night. The bustard killed Maddy! And I know who did it, Reg! I know who the murderer is!'

He put his hand over his mouth. But there was no time for shock. There was only time for action.

'We've got to nail this bustard, Reg. He's going to kill again, tomorrow! '

'B-b-but who is it, Jimmy? Who is Jack the R-R-Ripper?'

'For Chrissakes, Reg, keep your voice down!'

I pulled him back and spoke into his ear.

'You're not going to believe me. You're goin' to have to trust me on this. But it's . . .'

Even in profile I could see the desperately expectant

look on Reg's face. I knew it would change as soon as I said it.

'It's . . . the King.'

Reg turned and stared at me blankly.

'That's right, Reg. His Majesty. King George!'

Reg didn't say anything, but then I felt his body start to shake. He was laughing. He punched me in the arm harder than usual.

'Now I know yer p-p-pullin' me leg! The King! King George is Jack the Ripper!! Very f-f-flippin' amusin', I'm sure!'

'Gather round, men!' barked Sergeant Brough.

I'd have to explain to Reg later. I hated leaving it like that. I knew he'd be giving me funny looks for the rest of the day, like he was waiting for the punchline of some elaborate joke.

Sergeant Brough showed us how to aim and fire for real. We'd had the theory with mops, and now we were about to graduate. He demonstrated how to dig your elbows into the ground to steady and support the weight of the barrel. How to line up the sight correctly. How you should never tug at a trigger because it throws your aim out. How you should always squeeze gently.

Then it was our turn. We all had a go. It was exciting, and frightening. You could sense it in everyone: the awe.

How you can kill a man with a finger.

One squeeze of your finger.

'You c-c-can't be serious!'

Reg dropped the letter down on to the blanket, and

the candle flickered like it was annoyed, before steadying itself. We'd waited until all the men were asleep, but kept our voices down just in case.

'Face facts, Reg. The dates all match. And this letter practically spells it out.' I picked it up and held it to the light, pointing to the giveaway sentences.

'Look here . . . tellin' the newspaper editor to keep quiet . . . And God Save the King!'

Reg looked sceptical. 'But, Jimmy, it doesn't actu-ally s-s-say it was the K-K-King did it. It does look s-s-suspicious, mind. But you c-c-can't be s-s-sure. Not from this.'

'Come on, Reg, open your eyes! We knew it 'ad to be someone powerful, really powerful. You said that yerself. Who else could it be? The King has visited Portsmouth seven times since the war started, and he's murdered every time!'

'B-b-but that's not evidence. It's not p-p-proof.'

'Remember when I nearly got caught following the coppers to one of the murder scenes, when I was chasing the whistles? Well, I saw the King on a tram in Queen's Street. Bold as you like.'

I waited for it to sink in. Reg was staring at me.

'You s-s-saw the K-K-King on a tram in Queen's S-S-Street?' he repeated slowly, his mouth breaking into a wide smile. 'Did he have his c-c-crown and vermin r-r-robes on?'

'Be serious, Reg,' I said, 'and it's ermine, not vermin.'

'So you're tellin' me you s-s-saw the K-K-King

escaping from a m-m-murder, but it never crossed your mind to mention it to me b-b-before?'

Reg had a point.

'Well, I . . . er . . . I couldn't be *absolutely* sure.'

'And n-n-now you are?'

'Well, yes, Reg. Yes, I am. All the estimated dates of the murders tie up to around the time of his visits. Seven times. The last time was the day of my date with Maddy. But she didn't turn up. And you know why she didn't turn up, Reg? Cos that bustard King murdered her! And everybody's protecting him. Everybody wants to save the ruddy King.'

Reg still looked sceptical.

'If we don't stop 'im, there'll be another. Tomorrow. And another. And he'll go on and on and on, killing ordinary people. Unless he's stopped. We've got to stop him for Maddy's sake. And for all the others he's murdered.'

Reg shook his head, but I could tell he was wavering.

'Look, Reg. Jop must have figured out it was the King. Why do you think he got rid of his medals? You know how proud he was of them, Reg. Of fighting for King and country. Why else would he get rid of them? I tell you, he couldn't stomach wearin' 'em any more, cos he knew. He knew! He actually said he was ashamed of his King and country!'

Reg was still shaking his head.

'Do you remember what he said? Don't trouble trouble unless trouble troubles you. Well, seven women murdered is trouble. They're our people, Reg. We're at war.

It's time to do something about it. It's time to trouble trouble. That's what he meant. Now is the time. Time to go to war.'

'But s-s-supposin' you are right. What c-c-can we do about it? I mean, we're goin' to flippin' F-F-France on F-F-Friday!'

'I've got a plan . . .'

'I w-w-was afraid you were g-g-goin' to say that, Jimmy.'

' . . . And it's a bit risky, and it might not work.'

'Why d-d-does that not s-s-surprise me?' said Reg wearily.

'I knew I could rely on you, Reg.'

Chapter Twenty-seven

The dark alley was partly blocked by piles of old newspapers and rotting rubbish. A movement from deep
within made Reg and me jump. We laughed, nervously.
We wouldn't normally be spooked by feasting rats. Even
more intimidating was the deep thumping of the presses
coming from the newspaper offices that backed on to
the alley. Empty beer bottles and broken glass vibrated
and rattled on the ground with every rhythmic thump.
Reg and I trod carefully until our eyes got used to the
darkness. We could see the warm glow from the window
up ahead.

We made our way through the rubbish, kicking it and
sending the rats scurrying, until we were standing beneath
the frosted window. Reg cupped his hands together and
stooped down. I lifted my army boot into the cradle he
had made and Reg stood up, hoisting me high enough
to see inside, through the open top window. There was
a familiar smell but no smoke, and I knew instantly that
Mr Ralphs wasn't in his office. Launching myself head
first, I clambered in, knocking over something hard and
metallic. It clanged on the floor and Reg hissed at me.

'If you're g-g-gonna make a noise, Jimmy, d-d-do it in time with the f-f-flippin' th-th-thumpin'!'

'It's OK, Reg,' I whispered, picking up a polished cup that I'd knocked off a pedestal. It was now dented out of shape, an uneven oval instead of round. I tried to press it back but there was no way it was going to give. I read the inscription:

AWARDED BY THE REGIONAL
NEWSPAPER ASSOCIATION TO
Ebenezer Ralphs
OF THE
Whitechapel Gazette
IN RECOGNITION OF HIS
ACHIEVEMENT IN JOURNALISM
1888

Reg tapped on the bottom window. I released the catch so that he could climb in.

'You s-s-sure he ain't around? I c-c-can s-s-smell 'im.'

Reg was right. The room stank of tobacco smoke, and it was then I spotted Mr Ralphs's briar pipe on his desk. A thin milky-white wisp of smoke rose from the bowl. Reg and I looked at each other. Mr Ralphs was very close by.

I balanced the badly dented trophy back on the wooden pedestal.

Reg was worried. 'Do you think he'll n-n-notice?'

'Only if he looks at it.'

Suddenly the room shook with a piercing, drilling sound. Reg and I jumped in terror before realizing that it was Mr Ralphs's telephone. We'd never heard one actually ringing before. We don't have telephones in Portsea. In Portsea, if you want to talk to someone far away, you shout.

'Jesus, Reg! Quick! Hide!' I looked around desperately for somewhere to hide. 'Quick, under the desk!'

We crawled under the desk in the leg space between the drawer cabinets. It was deep enough for both of us. We just had to hope that Mr Ralphs wouldn't sit at his desk and stretch his legs.

As soon as we reached safety, crouching with our knees under our chins, the door opened and we knew from the hacking cough that it was Mr Ralphs. The coughing and the ringing stopped as the receiver was picked up.

'Ralphs here ... oh, good evening, or should I say morning, sir ... I trust you are happy with our handling of the matter ... Yes, sir. The lid is being kept firmly on this. Everything is being dealt with. You and your superiors can rely on us completely, here at the *Portsmouth Times*.'

There was a long silence, broken by what sounded like kissing. Reg and I looked at each other as thick smoke from the revived pipe began to tumble down and fill the lower part of the room. Reg held his hand over his mouth to stifle a cough.

'Good heavens! ... I mean ... my goodness ... me? ... of course ... well, I am deeply, deeply honoured, sir ... It has been a great privilege ... no, thank YOU, sir. Good night.'

Mr Ralphs replaced the receiver and walked around his

office. Reg and I followed his shoes with our eyes. Nice shoes. Expensive. Probably no change from seven guineas.

Mr Ralphs cleared his throat and spoke in a grand voice. 'Sir Ebenezer Ralphs!'

There was another kissing sound as he sucked on his pipe.

'SIR Ebenezer!'

Reg and I looked at each other. He was talking to himself in different posh voices, each one emphasizing the word 'Sir'. He was trying them out, to see which one fitted.

'SIR Ebenezer Ralphs' . . . kiss . . . 'Arise, SIR Ebenezer Ralphs' . . . kiss . . . 'SIR Ebenezer Ralphs is cordially invited to a Royal Garden Party at Buckingham Palace' . . . kiss . . . 'His Majesty requests the pleasure of the company of SIR Ebenezer Ralphs at the Royal War Victory Celebration at Windsor Castle' . . . kiss . . .

Reg had overcome his desire to cough with a desire to throw up. Nobody mimed vomiting better than Reg.

After a few minutes Mr Ralphs ran out of ways he could say his new honour. He put on his coat and made his way to the door, stopping to say, 'SIR Ebenezer Ralphs,' one last time while admiring himself in a mirror. On the way out we watched him stop and stare at his nameplate on the door for a few seconds. He smiled smugly then shut it behind him. Reg and I breathed a sigh of relief, crawled out towards the window and breathed in fresh oxygen.

'What a b–b–bustard! SIR Ebenezer B–B–Bustard! Sir Lyin' B–B–Bustard. SIR Lick-Arse Ebenezer Crawling

Crap-faced Lyin' B-B-Bustard! Stick that on yer door and smoke it, ya b–b–bustard!'

'You don't like 'im, do you, Reg?'

Reg composed himself and smiled. 'D–d–don't know what gave you that idea, Jimmy.'

The thumping sound of the presses became more urgent as we opened the door and checked that the corridor was clear. I don't know about Reg, but my heartbeat was racing, harder and faster. We edged our way along, past the mayors and councillors and past former editors of the paper who gazed their disapproval from their frames on the walls. We had to be careful. The thumping noise would mask any sound of approaching footsteps.

We came to the door marked 'TYPESETTING DEPARTMENT' and watched through the window. Two men were working at incredible speed, reading from sheets of paper that they took from trays on their left, then deftly picking letters from wooden frames and placing them in order on a block in front of them. They were big men, which made what they were doing look even more difficult and delicate, reminding me of Mr Vosbrugh and his skills with an icing nozzle.

'Tomorrow's news,' I whispered.

'Tomorrow's flippin' l–l–lies,' Reg corrected me.

We watched as the men finished their blocks and deposited them through a small hatch, before picking another article and starting another job.

'W–w–what do we do now?' asked Reg.

'Just wait,' I replied confidently. 'You keep lookout.'

In fact I wasn't confident at all. My plan could fall apart at any moment.

Gradually the trays emptied, and when they were clear the two men spoke to each other, glanced at the clock and headed for the door. Reg and I slipped around the corner of the corridor and watched them leave. They both took packages of what looked like their supper or breakfast or whatever meal it is you have in the early hours when you work all night.

'Quick, Reg! Go!'

The seat was still warm. The frame of letters was frightening. Different sizes. Different types. And they were all back to front. My heart sank. It was too much.

I froze.

'C-c-come on, Jimmy! We can d-d-do this! Where's our article?'

I took the piece of paper out of my breast pocket, unfolded it and laid it out flat on the bench.

'I'll keep a lookout while you p-p-pulls off the letters and then s-s-sets them, Jimmy. Right?'

I snapped out of it. 'Right, Reg!'

Reg never liked anything to do with printed words or reading or writing. He could read a bit, but that was about it. So it was down to me. It was like a school exam, except I didn't know how much time I had to do it in. But one thing was certain: if I didn't get a pass, more people would die. And the only thing I'd ever passed in my life till now was piss.

★

After a few minutes I started to get the hang of it. The letters were as cold and heavy as bullets, but they slotted in easily. I did large letters for the headline and found blank ones for the spaces between the words. But then I realized.

'Damn.'

'W-w-what's up, Jimmy?'

'I've done everything arse about face. You have to set type back to front, otherwise it prints in reverse.'

Reg nodded knowingly. 'I d-d-don't know what you're t-t-talkin' about, Jimmy.'

I emptied the tray and started again. My heart was beating in time with the presses. The clock on the wall said we'd already been there ten minutes. Now, concentrate. Right to left, K, then an I then an N then a G then a blank then a G . . .

Suddenly Reg grabbed my arm and the metal letters from the frame scattered noisily over the stone floor.

'What the heck are you playing at, Reg . . . !'

'Down, Jimmy, q-q-quick! There's someone outside, coming this way! Can't you hear him whistling?'

Reg pulled me behind the bench as the door slowly swung open and the tuneless whistling became audible above the thumping presses. But there was no point in hiding; as soon as the typesetters approached, we'd be rumbled. The bench legs offered no real cover. Nobody could miss our arses sticking out like two nervous herons. And they were big blokes. With meaty-thick arms and fists as big as a Grubb's ham. We didn't have a hope.

★

There was a strange shuffling sound, accompanied by the whistling, which gradually got louder and louder. Any second now. I looked at Reg in desperation. He held up two fingers defiantly and gestured in the direction of the sound, then crossed them for luck.

I closed my eyes, bracing myself for the inevitable.

I held my breath.

The whistling stopped.

'Evenin', chaps! Not having a good one, I can see! What a mess!'

The feet shuffled past the bench without stopping, kicking some of the scattered letters that lay in their path. Well-worn shoes, inferior brown leather. The voice of an old man, and the feet of an old man.

I smiled. I realized they belonged to the night messenger who'd taken us to the editor's office the previous day. I could see and feel the relief on Reg's face that it wasn't the burly typesetters, but panic set in as I struggled to think what to do next. The old man had mistaken us for the typesetters groping around on the floor for the dropped type.

One of us had to say something, and Reg's stutter would be a giveaway. I pulled in my chin and tried to sound like a typesetter, deep and gruff.

'Evenin'!'

Reg put his hand over his mouth to stifle a laugh.

'I would help you chaps down there, but at my age it could prove a one-way trip!' He chuckled as only old people do, and I laughed deeply, prodding Reg to do the same. With chins in, we rocked from side to side, helping to keep the laughter going. All the time we were laughing we wouldn't have to make conversation. We were jolly typesetters enjoying a joke, ho, ho, ho!

The shuffling stopped and I risked a quick look over the top of the bench. The old man delivered some papers into the printer's tray. I ducked down just as he turned, and he began his shuffle back to the door, sending more letters across the floor.

'See you later, chaps! Mind your ps and qs!'

He chuckled again, and Reg and I grunted a deep, typesetter's grunt and the door swung closed.

We stood up, looked at each other then looked at the floor. There was metal type everywhere. We looked up at the clock. The typesetters had been gone fifteen minutes. If they had a half-hour break, we only had another quarter of an hour to do what we came to do. We didn't say a word. There was no time to lose.

Reg got on his knees, filled his cupped hands with type and began making a pile on the bench. I sorted and picked letters out and placed them in the printing block. Meanwhile, the presses thumped on, marking time, counting down.

I patted down the final letter and admired my effort.

'Finished!'

It didn't seem much for the time it had taken, and it was difficult to read properly back-to-front, but it said what Reg and I wanted to say.

'Quick, Jimmy! Quick! They're c–c–coming back!'

Reg was at the door, frantically waving me over. I snatched up the filled block and stacked it with the others waiting to be printed, catching a glance at the whirring presses through the hatch, turning ink and paper into tomorrow's lies. I paused with a thought. It would make Jop's day to see some truth in tomorrow's morning edition.

'What you d-d-doin', Jimmy, the b-b-bleedin' cross-word?! We g-g-got to g-g-go now!'

The presses and my heartbeat were racing faster than ever as we ran down the corridor, reaching the corner just in time to look back and see the two typesetters close the door behind them.

We retraced our steps to Mr Ralphs's office and climbed up out of the window, using the trophy pedestal as a foothold. It was not until we were back on the street and making our way to the tram stop that we relaxed.

'Well, Reg, we did it. We flippin' well did it!'

'Yeah, Jimmy! That's gonna s-s-stuff the King!'

'Well and truly! What do you reckon on Mr Ralphs' chance of getting his knighthood now?'

'A b-b-bit less than b-b-bugger-all!'

We laughed long and hard as we skipped along the road. My army boots felt as if they weren't there. I almost felt like I was a barefoot mudlark again, with nothing to worry about. But at the back of my mind was the thought of what lay ahead. On the one hand, they couldn't touch us for what we had done because there was no way they could trace us. On the other, even if

216

they did, what could they do to us? We were being sent to France in a couple of days.

The first tram of the morning took us back to Portsdown Hill, and if it hadn't been for the conductor waking us up we'd never have made it back to camp in time for reveille.

Chapter Twenty-eight

The signal was given by a sentry on the western ridge of Portsdown Hill. The red flag waved in an arc against the grey sky on the horizon. Sergeant Brough spotted the signal, gave the order to fall in, and the men fell in like real soldiers. There was an edge that hadn't been there before and you could see the look of pride on Sergeant Brough's face. And Reg and I were as alert and as smart as everyone else, even though neither of us had had any sleep.

Suddenly a motor car approached, crunching gravel. The engine purred power, coping comfortably with the steep gradient of the hill road. It appeared, black and immaculate, and swung smoothly through the gates and into the camp. Clouds in the sky flashed by, reflected in the polished side-panels with silver trim.

I should have guessed it earlier. I was stupid. We knew it must be someone powerful. Someone more powerful than the police. You can't get more powerful than him.

He killed Poll and five other sisters. And, the last time, the last time he was in Portsmouth, he killed Maddy.

I hadn't understood. I thought she'd stood me up. But she'd put on her best dress and had left home to meet me at the Swiss Caff. It was the day of his seventh visit to the town. Seven visits, seven murders. She hadn't made it. While I was sitting there, drinking tea, Maddy was being murdered. Everyone was protecting him. But he had to be stopped before he killed again. Next time it could be anyone. It could be your mum. It could be mine.

But soon the morning edition of the *Portsmouth Times* would hit the streets, and everyone in Portsmouth would know. Word would spread all round the country. The man who sits on the throne, His Majesty King George the Fifth, the head of the British Empire is . . . a murderer. And no ordinary murderer. Jack the Ripper. The whole world would know it, and he would be finished.

The driver got out and opened the door, and a man swung himself out, straightened his uniform and was saluted by three generals.

He looked just like a normal human being. Yes, he got out of a posh car. And he had a fancier uniform and more medals than anyone else. But apart from that he could have been the strange man at number 21, or Mrs Griffin's lodger or the shipwright with the French cigarettes in Fog Corner. Except he wasn't.

He was Jack the Ripper.

I could see the medals glinting on his chest. He was smiling. Every time he came to Portsmouth, he murdered a woman. Is that why he gave himself medals? One for

each victim? And he was smiling. I couldn't get over that
smile.

The generals started to lead the man over to us, await-
ing inspection. I wanted to shout at him, tell him what
a bustard he was. Oy, King. You're a bustard. I felt my
breathing deepening.

Reg could tell I was getting angry. 'He's t-t-taller than
he looks on the s-s-stamps,' he whispered, still staring
straight ahead, 'but not as big as he should be. What
d-d-do you think, Jimmy?'

I smiled. 'I think you've just saved me from being
court-martialled, Reg.'

And then I started laughing and Reg joined in.
Sergeant Brough spotted us and glared.

The King spoke to some of the top brass and he barely
glanced at us, the men who were actually going to be
doing the fighting. One of the generals turned and called
on the men to give three cheers for the King. The Hip
Hip Hoorays boomed out and I wondered if they could
be heard down in the town, where people would be
getting their morning newspapers about now. Reg and I
stayed tight-lipped. We weren't even going to mime the
words, like we do to the hymns for the army chaplain.

The general then granted all men four hours' leave in
the name of the King, and the men renewed their cheers.
The King then sat back in his car and was gone.

I'd forgotten about that tradition. It was one of the
reasons why royal visits were so popular among soldiers
and sailors in the barracks and camps. I wasn't about to be

grateful, though. It was no good to Reg and me, because our mums would be at work. If it had been a whole day, we could have seen them one last time before we were sent to fight. At least we could go and see Jop, and get a copy of the *Portsmouth Times* and see if our plan had worked.

The tide was in, so mudlarking in that glorious, black, welcoming mud was out of the question. It was probably just as well, what with our smart new uniforms. Reg and I walked up the pier towards Jop's pitch. Something seemed different. Was it the sound of our boots on the wooden deck of the pier? Then I realized that we weren't walking, we were marching. Along the planks in step. Left, right, left, right, left, right.

'No, you can't 'ave yer bleedin' money back. What do you think I am, a bleedin' charity?'

Something wasn't right. We got closer. It wasn't Jop. There was another old man sitting on Jop's upturned crate with a pile of *Portsmouth Times* and a bottle of cider at his side. He didn't have a wooden leg and he didn't have Jop's philosophy that the customer is always right, even when he's wrong. The man standing in front of him was a red-faced naval lieutenant. He angrily threw the newspaper over the railings and into the sea and steamed past Reg and me, muttering, 'Treasonable trash!'

'W-w-where's J-J-Jop?' Reg looked worried.

I had a bad feeling. 'Let's ask.'

I held a penny out for a paper. I could smell the rough

cider on the old man's breath. He snatched the penny, studied it, then threw a copy at me. There was none of Jop's deft folding, slick delivery or smiling banter.

'We were expecting to see Jop. Do you know where he is?'

The old man looked up, surprised to see us still there.

'No.'

He picked up his cider bottle and had a swig, indicating that the conversation was over.

'Do you know who I'm talking about? Jop? This is his pitch.'

The old man scowled. ''S my bleedin' pitch.'

Reg and I looked at each other.

'But what happened to Jop? He's been here forever.'

The old man smiled and rubbed his finger and thumb together under my nose.

'He w-w-wants m-m-money,' mumbled Reg, handing him a shilling. The old man pocketed it and held out his hand for more. I gave him a handful of coppers. He put them away safely and smiled.

'He's bleedin' dead.'

Reg covered his mouth and I felt a surge of anger.

'What? . . . How?'

The old man made the money sign again. Reg shook his head. I could see tears in his eyes, and it was only the anger that was stopping mine. I got another shilling out and handed it over. Another smile flickered across his face.

'The cough carried him off.' He chuckled and took a

long, hard swig from his bottle. The glugging sound made me want to hit him.

Reg and I walked back up the pier, silently. Above us, seagulls cried as they soared high. Jop had been a good man. A decent man. And a good soldier. I remembered what he'd said when the *Good Hope* had sunk. About seagulls being sailors' souls and rats being soldiers'. And that he'd be a rat soon. I felt the tears dropping on to my uniform. Jop was free now. Free as the wind.

It was between Dockyard shifts, so we were alone when we got to Fog Corner. It was strange going in there, in our army boots, not having to watch out for cigarette ends, broken tobacco tins and gobs of spit.

'Jop was a champion gobber.'

'The b-b-best.'

We sat on the benches and breathed in the familiar smell of stale smoke. Then we noticed each other's tear stains down the front of our new uniforms. I don't know who started laughing first, but soon we were both laughing deeper than corporation drains.

'D-d-don't look g-g-good, do it? Two big, w-w-wet babies!'

'Brave warriors! Jop would be having a laugh! He'd probably present us with his white feather!'

We laughed again until the tears came and went.

I looked at the newspaper in my lap. It didn't take long to spot our story, even though it had been slotted in the third column at the bottom of the page. The words leapt out at me. My hands started shaking. I read it out for Reg:

KiNg GeORGE
iS
JocK THE RippER

King George has killeb seVen women in Portsmouth since the war starteb.

HE murbers one woman each time he visits the town. Added to the murbers in WhitEchapel in 1880s, this makes at least 12 murbers. He must be stoppeb. The police and newspapers are Covering it up, so it's down to evrydoby else to stoq him. Don't be fooleb. Just because he's a kiNg don't mean he's not caqadle of murber. He's a toTal mabman.

Reg nodded approvingly and smiled. 'W-w-we've done our duty. Jop would have l-l-loved to have s-s-seen it.'

'Yeah. A little bit of truth in a newspaper, for once.'

'One thing, J-J-Jimmy.' Reg pointed to the headline. 'Who's *Jock* the R-R-Ripper?'

Damn, he'd noticed.

'Come on, Reg. I was under a lot of pressure. Everyone will know what we mean.'

'Sh-sh-should put a s-s-stop to the m-m-murders.'

'If this doesn't do it, nothing will.'

★

We went back down to the shoreline and skimmed stones; but I don't know what it was, the way we were feeling, the stiffness of the uniform, whatever it was, we didn't seem very good at it any more. My world record, verified by Jop, was safe.

Suddenly, in the midst of an average seven-bouncer, there was shouting from the pier. I looked up, expecting to see Jop, but it was an angry voice. It was the old man. Two policemen were picking up his pile of newspapers. The old man swore and struggled with them, but he was pushed away. He shook his cider bottle and swore at them again.

The policemen ignored him and carried the bundles towards the pierhead, where a corporation refuse horse-and-cart was waiting. The old man carried on shouting, but then he sank out of sight, clutching his cider bottle like a baby to his chest.

'What d-d-do you think that w-w-was all about?' asked Reg.

'Looks like they're trying to get as many newspapers back from sellers as they can, to limit the damage. My guess is, they're taking them to the incinerator.'

'B-b-but surely they'll have sold thousands already? They c-c-can't keep it quiet.'

'You're right, Reg. The cat's out of the bag. It's gone too far.'

Chapter Twenty-nine

Sergeant Brough struck a lucifer and stoked up his first pipe of the evening. It was our last night in England, or Blighty as we call it. The smoke billowed out and quickly filled the tent.

'You know, I should've put you both on a charge for laughing and for not joining in the three cheers for His Majesty yesterday. People could interpret that as some sort of snub.'

Reg did his mock innocent act. 'Can we help it if we were s-s-suddenly struck dumb, Sarge?'

Sergeant Brough laughed. 'Yeah. Between you and me, royalty has that effect on me too. Seems to have done the men some good, though. Nobody seems to believe that bizarre story in yesterday's paper that everyone's been talking about. The country's gone mad. There's even been questions in the House.'

'Whose h-h-house?' asked Reg.

'Why is it bizarre?' I found myself almost getting angry. 'I mean, why couldn't King George be Jack the Ripper? There was a murder each time he visited Portsmouth! Doesn't anyone think that's suspicious?!'

I didn't mean it to come out so forcefully, and Sergeant Brough looked taken aback.

'Steady on, lad. It just seems far-fetched to me. And anyway, according to this,' he held up the afternoon edition, 'the editor has been arrested. Apparently he's a prime suspect for the alleged seven murders! The police found out he was a reporter in Whitechapel when the original Jack the Ripper murders took place. They reckon he must have started murdering again in Portsmouth and made a half-cocked attempt to blame the King! Can you believe that? Trying to frame the King! That's treason. He'll be shot for that alone.'

Reg and I looked at each other. I think I had the same look of panic on my face as he did.

'Sh-sh-sh-sh-shot?' Reg could hardly say the word, and it wasn't because of his stutter.

Things were going seriously wrong. Nobody believed the King was guilty, and now the wrong man had been arrested!

Sergeant Brough noticed the change in Reg and me. He knew something was wrong but couldn't put his finger on it.

'Of course he'll be shot! If calling the King a mass murderer isn't treason, I don't know what is! He'll be taken to the Tower of London and shot. And he won't be the first or last to face a firing squad in this war.'

My panic turned to guilt. This was my fault. What could I do to put it right?

'Anyway,' Sergeant Brough continued, 'the men'll go off tomorrow happy, raring to fight for their King and country. What will you two be fightin' for?'

Reg composed himself enough to give a shrug. 'To s-s-survive. That's what it's all about, isn't it, S-S-Sarge?'

Sergeant Brough withdrew his pipe and nodded. 'That's the bottom line.' He cupped the bowl in his palm and felt the heat. 'You've just got to keep your heads down. Don't worry about what's happening at home.'

But I realized that Reg and I had no choice. We couldn't just keep our heads down. We had to prove it was the King in order to stop any more murders and to stop Mr Ralphs being executed.

'Sarge. It is the King.' I took the letter out of my pocket and handed it to him. 'Look. Here's proof.'

There was a long silence while he unfolded it and studied it closely, his pipe aiding his concentration. He read it and reread it, nodding, and eventually withdrew the pipe from his mouth.

'You're right, lad. This proves there's been a cover-up. And it goes to the top. High up in the government.'

There was no stopping us now. We explained about the number of royal visits and the number of murders. I explained how I thought I'd seen the King in the tram in Queen's Street. And how Maddy, my Maddy, was murdered on the last day the King had come to the town. And how Jop felt like spitting on his medals because he said he was disgusted with his King and country.

Sergeant Brough handed back the letter.

'In the circumstances, some of that sounds almost plausible, lads, but I'm afraid you're way off the mark. It wasn't the King who did the murders.'

'But you just said we were right! You said there'd been a cover-up!' I didn't understand.

Suddenly, there was a muffled rap on the canvas door-flap. Colonel Jarvis entered and we all stood to attention. He exchanged salutes with Sergeant Brough but didn't seem to notice Reg and me.

'Sergeant. There are two men in our camp from the Fingerprint Bureau of Scotland Yard. The General has given them permission to set up in the canteen to take the fingerprints of all the men in the three Hampshire battalions. It's a complete waste of bloody time, I know, but it has to be done. They're being supervised by a man from the counter-espionage unit. Arrange the details as soon as possible, would you? It will take all night, but it can't be helped. '

'Yes, sir.'

The Colonel turned to leave, but Sergeant Brough wanted to find out more.

'What's it all about, sir?'

'National security. Between you and me, there have been some new developments in the newspaper treason case.' He lowered his voice, but Reg and I could still hear. 'The editor was with the Mayor when one of the killings took place, so he's in the clear. No question. But two soldiers of the Hampshire Regiment – or rather, one hopes, Hun saboteurs dressed as two of our men – were seen acting suspiciously near the newspaper offices. And coincidentally, two shifty-looking soldiers visited the editor the previous day. Bloody queer business.'

Sergeant Brough looked thoughtful. 'I see.'

'The men from the Fingerprint Bureau are trying to match fingerprints left on the metal type used for that bloody treacherous article. These people from London know their onions. And, by God, they're bloody tenacious! I'd hate to be in the shoes of whoever's responsible. But they deserve everything that's coming to them, eh, Sergeant? Murder's bad enough, but trying to discredit the regiment is bloody unforgivable!'

Sergeant Brough shot us a wink.

'Yes, sir. Shooting's too bloody good for them!'

The Colonel hurrumphed in agreement and marched out of the tent.

Reg and I looked at each other. And Sergeant Brough looked at us, suddenly all serious.

'You lads haven't got something to tell me, have you?'

Chapter Thirty

'What do you mean, Sarge?' I knew it was a waste of time denying it, but that wasn't about to stop me trying.

Sergeant Brough raised an eyebrow. 'Would it save everyone a lot of trouble if I took you both over to the canteen and got you fingerprinted first?'

Reg and I looked at each other. The game was up.

'You m-m-might as well just sh-sh-shoot us, and have done with it.' Reg was holding back the tears.

'I'm afraid . . . you're probably right.' Sergeant Brough looked seriously worried.

'But if we can prove the King is Jack the Ripper . . .'

'No!' Sergeant Brough's concern turned to anger. He jabbed his finger at me. 'You got it wrong. WRONG! And what you did was treason. A capital offence. Make no mistake. You slander the King and you undermine the British war effort. No. There will be no mercy. You will be tried and shot . . .'

An idea was forming in his head.

'Unless . . .'

'Unless w-w-what, S-S-Sarge?'

'Unless you disappear from the battalion personnel list. They can't expect to fingerprint you if they don't know you exist!'

If I were choosing a hiding place, the floor of the camp latrines would not be at the top of my list. They were not called the bogs for no reason. There was a row of them, outdoors, with no roof, each cubicle separated by temporary wooden walls and a flimsy door that you couldn't lock. They were designed to be easily dismantled, moved and reassembled wherever the camp went.

Reg and I tried breathing through our mouths, but the stench was still worse than the police cells, Fog Corner, the sewage outlet at Eastney on a hot day and Mr Ralphs's pipe tobacco, all rolled into one. But it was Sarge's idea, and it might just save our skins. He hung an 'OUT OF ORDER' sign on the door and hurried off to arrange the roll-call. He figured he could retype the two pages of names where Reg's and my name appeared. It was this alphabetical list that the roll-call would be made from. He would then give it to the fingerprint men for them to work their way through. That was the plan.

Reg and I stared up at the night sky. I yawned wide and hard, setting Reg off. The stars looked like pinpricks in a suffocating black blanket, and when they flickered I imagined someone behind that blanket looking down on what us little people were doing. I get stupid thoughts like that when I'm tired. We hadn't slept for two long days. There wasn't much room, but we curled up on the ground each side of the toilet bowl.

232

'Do you think S-S-Sarge's plan will w-w-work?' whispered Reg.

'I don't know, Reg, but it's his best shot. All we can do is lie here and wait.'

'We've g-g-got ourselves in a right m-m-mess, haven't we, Jimmy?'

'Yeah, Reg.' I didn't know what else to say. 'I'm sorry, Reg. I wish none of this had happened. I'm ... I'm sorry.'

'S-s-sorry? What you t-t-talking about, Jimmy?'

But I knew it was all my fault, and I knew Reg knew it was my fault. But he wasn't showing it. He made an exaggerated sniff and screwed up his face.

'I t-t-tell you what, if your average B-B-British soldier's aim with a rifle is as g-g-good as his aim at p-p-pissing, we're all done for anyway.'

The last thing I remember was laughing until my eyes closed, and then nothing mattered. Nothing could touch us.

It was the barking that did it. Some way away. And men shouting. 'Over there! They're on to them!'

I opened my eyes. The black blanket was gone.

Reg was already awake. He was holding his finger to his lips. 'It's the military police! And they've got dogs!' he whispered, watching them through the crack in the door between the hinges. 'They're heading this way!'

I looked through the crack.

Two dog-handlers with bloodhounds on straining leads. And they were heading straight for us. Their tails whipped the air and strings of saliva hung down from their mouths. Each handler was clutching something in his other hand. They got closer, and I realized they were using our blankets for scent. Three big military policemen with drawn revolvers jogged behind them. Followed by Sergeant Brough.

'Christ, Reg! Sergeant Brough has bloody well shopped us! The bustard! We're gonna have to make a run for it!'

'W-w-what, and get sh-sh-shot in the back? No, Jimmy. We'll sit t-t-tight.'

'But we're gonna get shot anyway, Reg! They're coming for us!'

'You're wrong about S-S-Sarge. S-s-something must have g-g-gone wrong with his p-p-plan last night. He'll think of s-s-something. T-t-trust him.'

The dogs were getting closer, we could hear their excited panting.

'Don't be stupid, Reg! We have to make a run for it! This is our only chance! Come on!!'

I reached for the door catch. Suddenly I felt a violent jolt. It took a few seconds to realize what was happening. Reg's face was an inch away from mine. All I could see were his eyes. And they were angry.

'Shhhhhuttt the heck up!!!!' he hissed. 'We're staying here!'

For a moment, the dogs and the guns didn't matter. The last time I saw Reg like this, it ended in a brutal fight with Archie. I was so shocked, there was no question of me arguing. It was too late anyway. He'd blown our only chance.

Reg put his finger to his lips. The search party stopped outside, a few feet away. The bloodhounds sniffed and whimpered and their tails drooped.

'The dogs have lost the scent,' came a voice. 'Have the latrines been searched?'

Reg and I backed away from the crack and looked at each other. The game was up.

'Yes. I did it myself,' replied Sergeant Brough.

'What about that one with "OUT OF ORDER" on the door?'

'I checked all of them personally, and I wish I hadn't! You really don't want to go in there!'

There was loud, knowing laughter.

'Right, men, let's try the ablutions block!'

Reg and I looked through the crack, to see them heading towards the washrooms. I closed my eyes and breathed a sigh of relief. But, not far behind, was a feeling of utter shame. Shame for not trusting the Sarge, and shame for not trusting Reg.

Sergeant Brough appeared an hour or so later and shut the door behind him. He was holding two bulging kitbags, which meant the cubicle was now so cramped we had to stand to attention.

'They've gone now. They're concentrating their search on the town. They're convinced you're there. By God, that was a close shave! I thought those dogs had you!'

'Saved by the smell!' I joked.

'Saved by Sarge, more like,' corrected Reg.

'Yes, Sarge. I don't know what to say. Except, er, thanks.'

'Sorry, it didn't work out the way I planned it.' Sarge explained, 'They had their own personnel records from headquarters, so they knew there were two men missing. And it didn't take them long to find out who you are and where you live.'

I thought about Mum, and I hoped they wouldn't upset or hurt her.

'W-w-what are we gonna do, Sarge? I mean, where c-c-can we hide?'

'We're finished,' I said, 'unless we can convince everyone that the King is the murderer.'

Sergeant Brough faced me. 'I told you before. It's not the ruddy King!'

'But it's our only hope!'

'It is NOT the King. Get that idea out of your head, will you?' said Sarge firmly.

'But how can you be so sure?' I argued.

'It's only fair to tell you. I know who's responsible.'

Reg and I exchanged glances.

'All right, if it's not the K-K-King, then who is it, S-S-Sarge?'

Sergeant Brough looked at us both. It was like he was regretting what he had just said, and was wondering how to explain something.

'Do you remember what I told you about the Boer War? I've been in the army all my life. I know what some men are capable of.'

Reg was getting impatient. 'But who, S-S-Sarge? Who?'

My mind was working hard, searching for logic, searching for truth.

Sergeant Brough clenched the stem of his unlit pipe between his teeth.

'It's us.'

'US?'

Reg and I looked at each other. What was Sarge saying? I was beginning to wonder about his sanity. Us?

'Yes, us,' confirmed Sergeant Brough. 'By us, I don't mean us personally! I mean us, as in the army. And navy. Soldiers, sailors, marines.'

He paused for a few seconds to let it sink in.

'Since the war started there's been, I guess, forty thousand extra men in camps like this, barracks and billets throughout Portsmouth. There's always been the odd murder in the town, what with the navy being here all the time, but since the war they've multiplied. We're like an occupying army, and wherever there's an army, there's always a few madmen in the ranks who rape and murder.'

I wasn't having this.

'No. NO! What about the dates? That's no coincidence! It can't be! It must be the King!'

Sergeant Brough shook his head. 'The coincidental dates of the murders . . . well, they must tie in because of the traditional leave that servicemen get when royalty visits.'

Reg and I didn't say anything, we were too shocked. I needed so much to be right. My brain was trying desperately, hopelessly, to find arguments. But I knew that I had been wrong. So very, utterly wrong. How could anyone be so completely stupid?

The enormity of what we had done was beginning to register. Reg was looking at me in a strange way. Like he wanted to murder me.

Sergeant Brough didn't notice, but I was relieved that he was with us, standing between Reg and me.

'You're right about one thing: there's been a huge cover-up. The authorities obviously think it would be bad for morale if it was known that their brave Tommies and bluejackets were murdering townsfolk. So the police don't look for the men responsible, they just keep it quiet. If it ever got out, I guess they reckon people might get confused and not support the war. I reckon that's why you were picked up and ended up here. Sent off to fight. Conveniently out of the way.'

Now it was my turn to be angry. 'So it's all right for women like my mum and her sisters and Maddy to get murdered. Nobody's gonna stop it? Nobody cares?'

Sergeant Brough shrugged. It wasn't a shrug of not caring. It was a shrug I'd seen before. A shrug of desperation and powerlessness. And I knew then that my mum knew what he knew. She'd known all along. And Jop had worked it out too. He'd given up his medals in disgust. It wasn't the King bit of 'King and country' that he was disgusted with. It was the other bit. Or at least some of the people who were fighting for it. He didn't want to be a part of it any more.

Sergeant Brough scraped out the bowl of his pipe with his penknife and tapped it on the latrine wall.

Reg was still staring at me.

'All right, Reg. I know what you're thinking. And you're right. It's all my fault. I was wrong. Very wrong. I'm sorry.'

'S-s-sorry? Oh, that's all r-r-right then! That makes everything f-f-fine! We b-b-break into a newspaper office and f-f-falsely accuse His Majesty K-K-King George of being the most evil, n-n-nasty and vicious murderer in British history. Tens of thousands of p-p-people read it. And y-y-you're s-s-sorry?'

'What can I say, Reg?'

'And now w-w-we're Britain's most wanted criminals, on the r-r-run, with nowhere to go! Bloody hell, Jimmy, don't you understand? When they c-c-catch us, we'll be shot!'

Reg slumped down the wall and just sat there, staring at the ground, shaking his head.

Sergeant Brough looked sad. He reached into his breast pocket. 'I'm sorry, lads. This is all I can do for you. You've got to get out of the country. It's not safe in England.'

He handed us some papers and an army pay book each.

'This is your new identity. I've made them out in the names of two soldiers missing in action at Wipers. Most of the men from the Second Worcesters were either killed, wounded or are missing in action. Others were dispersed to other battalions, so if you turn up, they'll do the same to you. But you must be careful. Get rid of all evidence that you were in the Hampshire Regiment, and always, always refer to each other using your new names.'

Reg and I looked at the papers.

'B-b-but how are we going to get to F-F-France, Sarge?'

'Well, you wouldn't get very far if you tried to escape as part of this battalion, that's for sure. But the latrines are being crated up this morning . . .' Sarge winked. 'And nobody's going to notice an extra crate. I've put a crowbar in your kitbag so you can get yourselves out. It'll take two days, but there's enough grub and drink in there to last you.'

'Thanks, Sarge. How can we thank you for everything you've done?'

He smiled, pulled a flask out of his pocket and some mess tins out of the kitbags and poured out three drinks. He handed one each to Reg and me.

'Just survive, lads.' He held his tin up. 'To the two of you. Jimmy and Reg.'

'To us,' I corrected him. 'We weren't bad at being pains in the arse, were we?'

Sergeant Brough patted me on the shoulder and smiled. 'You did your best, son. That's all you can do. You've qualified as a lifelong member of the pain-in-the-arse club, no question.'

We clanked the mess tins together and gulped the contents down. I had only smelt whisky before, never drunk it. It felt like fire.

Reg and I both coughed, deep from the heart, and we all laughed.

Sergeant Brough looked us in the eye, from Reg to me and back again.

'You know, I'd be proud to 'ave both of you as sons. My sons.'

Reg and I didn't know what to say. I guess we were embarrassed. But I knew what to do. I held out my hand, and Sergeant Brough shook it firmly.

'Good luck, son.'

And then Reg did the same.

Chapter Thirty-one

Do you ever wonder how you ended up where you are? If you're anything like me, you only do it when things go wrong. When you're in a bit of a hole. Well, I'm doing it right now. Wondering how I ended up where I am. Because, as holes go, the one I'm in couldn't be bigger.

I have to write it down, to explain how it ended like this.

Not for anyone else, but for me. I guess I want to explain it to myself. How I ended up fighting on the same side as the enemy. The enemy who murder women in Portsea. The enemy who murder my mum's friends. The enemy who murdered Maddy.

But I hope someone else reads it as well, because it could be the only thing left.

I've nearly finished, now.

It's nearly time.

As I sit here, waiting, I can smell the black mud of the Somme. There are pieces of people sticking out of it, bone-white and blood-red.

I can feel the freezing mud clinging and pulling me down, as if it wants me to be part of it. As if it wants to absorb me.

I've been waiting for so long for the tide to wash away the death and the debris, but it just doesn't come.

Me and Reg went over the top three days ago but Reg hasn't come back yet. I'm still waiting.

I miss him.

I remember, once, Reg screamed back from the water's edge that he'd dug up a shell. I remember laughing and shouting, 'Polish it up and 'ang it round yer neck, yer big girly!'

And he glared at me. I can see his face now.

'No! Yer bustard,' he shouted, 'it's a bleedin' shell!'

Reg held up his shell. It was a shell. Of the silver-metal, unexploded kind.

'Jesus,' I said.

In a matter of seconds Reg and I were on the cobbled Hard, a hundred yards away, laughing our knackers off.

Here, on the Somme, there's nowhere to run. And I can't remember when I last laughed.

Jop was right about soldiers' souls. At night, when the shelling stops, no man's land comes alive. The earth looks like it's moving as thousands of black rats move together, in and out of the shell holes, and disappear into the trenches. Jop was right about so many things. He was a proud man and a proud soldier. He wanted the murderers

found. He didn't want us to give up looking for the
truth.

Here, on the Somme, shrapnel flies like lethal coins.
    It's time to wash the coins.
    I open my fist. Maddy's thruppenny piece. I close my
fist and clench it so hard, I can feel my nails pierce
my palm. But there's no pain.

Yes, shrapnel flies like lethal coins. It takes men's
heads off. It cuts men in half. It turns them into mud. The
murderers will not survive this. Cannot survive this. Their
souls will not survive.

As I wait for the whistle to blow, I'm thinking about
Pompey at Fratton Park with seconds to go. The
score doesn't matter. Who wins doesn't matter. Nothing
matters.

I don't want to be a mudlark any more.

I'm picking the dried mud off my trousers. If Mum
could see me now, she wouldn't be so proud. She'd tell
me off for getting so mucky and she'd reach for the
tin bath and carbolic. She'd pour the hot water down
my back.
    I can feel it now. Washing away my sins, she'd say.
    Wait.
    Don't breathe.
    I'm easing off what might be a world record. It's

coming ... Yes! It's here, in my hands, Reg will never believe it ... See.

The laws of nature can be defied.

I've proved it.

I'm smiling.

There's the whistle.

It's time.

Old Money
with its value and modern equivalents

a **farthing** – a quarter of an old penny
(about ten would equal 1p!)

thruppence or a **thruppenny bit** – three
old pence (just over 1p)

coppers – small change (pennies, halfpennies
and farthings, but also a slang word for the police!)

a **tanner** – six old pence (just over 2p)

a **shilling** or **bob** – twelve old pence (5p)

two bob – twenty-four old pence (10p)

half a crown – thirty old pence
(just over 12p)

a **ten-bob note** – 120 old pence (50p)

a **guinea** – twenty-one shillings
or 252 old pence (£1:10p)

John Sedden says . . .

This story was inspired by the true-life mudlarks who begged, scavenged and entertained in the mud of Portsmouth Harbour from Victorian days up until the middle of the last century.

By courtesy of *The News*, Portsmouth

The photograph above shows some mudlarks at Portsmouth in 1935 (and unusually shows an adult joining in). The lad on the left appears to have found a horn from an old wind-up phonograph (record player).

Affectionately named after the mudlark – a bird that feeds off creatures living in the mudflats – the boys and young men who took up mudlarking lived in the poorest slums of the Portsea district of Portsmouth, a stone's throw away from the harbour mud.

They waited, down in the black mud, ready to encourage holidaymakers, sailors and soldiers to toss coins from the railway pier. What made them different from the many street beggars of the port was their charm and their cheek and, of course, their antics in the mud.

But while they were popular with many visitors and locals alike, others were appalled by the spectacle. The police took a very dim view of their activities and made regular attempts to stop them. With little success.

Mudlark is set during the First World War. In this period there were several murders of working women in Portsmouth. These tragic events received little coverage in the local newspapers of the time, which were full of news about the war.

There are no reports of the murders having being solved.